DYING
STAR

BOOK ONE : PROPHECY

SAMSUN LOBE

 New Generation **Publishing**

For Erika

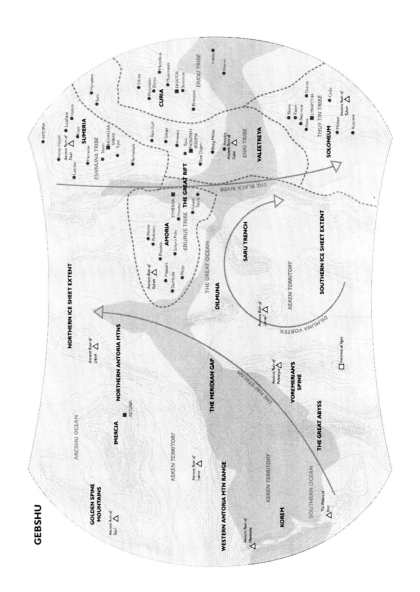

GEBSHU

SON GEBSHU

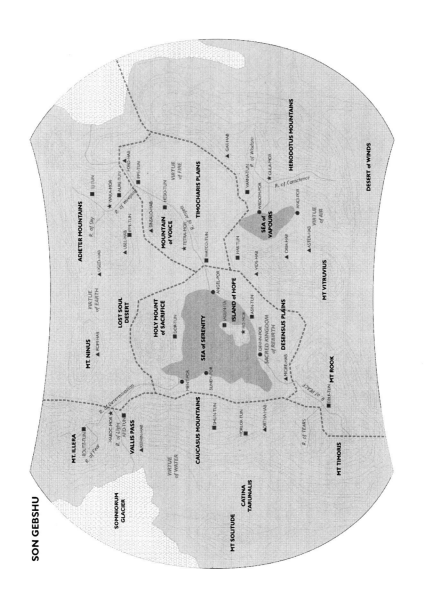

Prologue: The Great Flood

In the time of our ancient grandfathers, our planet Gebshu, basked in the light from our sacred star, Shu, and the peoples of our planet prospered. Our forebears lived on the land above the ocean surface in great cities of stone, breathing fresh air and feeling the heat of Shu on their skin.

Then the Emperor of the world and his magi discovered a 'new science' and unlocked the power within a mineral known as Lexan Stone. At first it was a great discovery and many wonders were worked. The greatest of all these feats was that of 'shimmer travel'. The resonating stone created a shimmering field through which objects were thrown, and then appeared miles from the original location. The technique was perfected so that people could travel through them over vast distances.

With this untold power at his disposal the Emperor declared himself a God. He outlawed the worship of the ancient deities, with the premise that if they truly existed they would make themselves known to him. He used the shimmer portals to take his armies to all parts of Gebshu where all tribes were forced to acknowledge him as the only true God. He destroyed or enslaved any that stood before him. The age of light had ended.

Before the Emperor's ascension there were believed to be many ancient gods controlling all aspects of the world - Povian the god of the ocean, Dalnu god of the land,

Ventnor the god of death and above all these the King of the Gods, ShumenRa who dwelled in the centre of Shu itself.

It was ShumenRa who finally answered the taunts of the Emperor. The great star Shu raged with fury and lances of light shot out into space; the colour of the great star changed from its dusky yellow to a bright white and with this change came fire and destruction.

The heat changed the weather on the surface of Gebshu and the land was engulfed by tornados and tsunamis. The land was torn apart and the mountains crumbled or spewed molten rock into the air. It was as if every god had awoken and declared war on the people of Gebshu. The storms and chaos lasted for many decades and millions died. The Emperor returned from his conquests and kept his loyal armies close. There was no longer a need for war, as survival had taken its place.

In the last months of the world the great ocean ice sheets melted and the world that had once breathed air was submerged beneath the roaring ocean. Legend tells that the Emperor and his loyal followers used the shimmer portals and escaped to the moon of Gebshu, Son-Gebshu. The peoples left behind were drowned in the Great Flood. The gods had cleansed the world.

A handful of faithful servants to the true gods survived and found a life beneath the surface of the water. The founding fathers of the Ocean tribes had understood the anger of ShumenRa, and they understood he had allowed them to live but never again bask in the glory of his presence, forever to remain beneath the surface of the ocean. And so began the Age of Half-Light.

Chapter 1 – The Lord Emperor

Muyda knew that something was wrong. It was normal for the Lord Emperor to summon her at a moment's notice, but ordinarily she would be notified by a palace guard and make her way there unaccompanied. This time, however, she was being led by Ty-Sem. Ty-Sem was one of seven select warriors who formed the personal bodyguard of the Emperor. They would not normally be asked to perform such a menial task as this.

Muyda followed in silence, her head bowed, trying to keep up with the great strides of Ty-Sem. He was a giant of a man even among the other warrior castes. He wore his black imperial ceramic armour as a badge of his position, the white sun emblem of the emperor embossed on the chest plate and the white symbols on the pawldrons indicating his position as a Dominator. His white cloak billowed behind him. It was covered in ancient writing, all prayers of some form to the God Emperor. At his side, strapped to his thigh, was a nail gun and strapped to his back were two falcatas.

Muyda remembered the day she had seen Ty-Sem on the training ground practising his sword movements. The two black-bladed falcatas both had white symbols etched into the length of the blades, and he had spun them in a black and white blur as he had executed his sword pattern. She remembered also how impressed she had been with the power, finesse and control he possessed; he was no less impressive this morning as he strode with a rhythmic chink along the corridor.

He opened a door that led them out into the Great Square. Muyda shielded her eyes from the light, she blinked to adjust her vision and hurried to keep step. Ty-Sem's bio-shield eye implants automatically darkened as the light touched them, his eyes turning black.

They passed through a series of high arches supported by massive pillars, all intricately engraved with scenes of conquests and legendary heroes. They came out into a smaller courtyard. At the other end of the open space the Imperial Palace stood like a dark obelisk threatening the sky itself. All of the buildings on Son-GebShu were constructed of black kullstone. Muyda thought it ironic that these buildings were supposed to portray the greatness of the Lord Emperor, but it looked more like a monolithic tombstone. Perhaps that was more fitting after all.

As they approached the gates of the palace the two warriors guarding the entrance touched their forearms to their chests and bowed their heads slightly to acknowledge the visitors. Ty-Sem lifted his gauntleted hand to the huge doors, which seemed to dwarf even him. They opened with ease, as if they weighed nothing at all. Security wasn't really an issue; there was seldom any trouble from the Dumonii or the nameless, and the entire city of Sagen-Ita was an unpenitrateable fortress built on top of an island that sat in the Sea of Serenity. Any trouble usually came from internal politics.

They walked on through the vast space of the nave. The roof was so high it was almost a blur. It made Muyda's head spin when she looked up at the massive scripted pillars that held the ceiling on flying buttresses way overhead. She had remembered the awe she had felt when she had first entered the temple. She had visited most of the temples on Son-Gebshu but all of them paled into insignificance against the majesty of the Holy Temple of the God Emperor. As they reached the end of the nave, she raised her head slightly to see who else had been summoned to the throne.

The throne was on the same scale as everything else in the temple; a huge black chair carved from a single piece of kullstone. It had religious markings engraved into its surface, and the relief detail had been picked out in brilliant white. The Lord Emperor Senn sat on the throne and despite its gigantic size he did not seem out of proportion. To the right of the Emperor stood Danus Venra. Muyda's heart sank and her stomach knotted. Whatever the reason for her summons it wasn't going to be good if Venra had anything to do with it.

Muyda and Venra had never seen eye to eye and Muyda knew of Venra's jealousy when she was pronounced Muyda Apos Senn; wife of the Emperor. Venra stood motionless, her head slightly bowed and the arm length hair spines that radiated around her skull made Muyda think of a desert lizard. She wore a white tunic decorated with script and prayers and showing far too much flesh than Muyda thought was acceptable for a woman of her station. On the left of the Emperor stood Principal Dar-Ota flanked by two more of the Dominators, Cam-Sem and Zo-Sem. All were silent; a macabre tableaux waiting for events to unfold. As they neared the dais Ty-Sem stopped, dropped to one knee and fervently slapped his vambrace across his chest. Muyda followed suit, dropping to both knees and bowing to touch her forehead onto the cold stone floor of the temple.

"Muyda Apos Senn, my Lord" announced Ty-Sem, his gruff voice cutting the tension like a serrated razor. Lord Senn rose from the throne, his massive bulk overshadowing all present. The Emperor's armour was painted completely white, it reflected the light and gave him an ethereal almost angelic aura. His white fur cloak pinned to his armour by icons of Shu, spilled out behind him onto the dais. He was truly a formidable man. He approached Ty-Sem and nodded to him. The Dominator took one step back and bowed his head once more and stood motionless like one of the statues flanking the Sanctuary.

"Arise my Lady" commanded the Emperor, his voice calm but with ultimate authority. Muyda rose, but kept her head bowed. It was not appropriate for a woman to look directly at the Emperor unless explicitly directed to do so. "Do you know why I have summoned you here?" asked Lord Senn.

"I am sure you have good reason my Lord, but I confess I am at a loss as to why." Muyda's voice was steady but she was struggling to control her nerves and the fear rising inside. She had always known in her heart that this day would come.

"I am sure that you are" he quizzically replied. He spun on his heel and faced the Principal. "Perhaps you could explain it to her my trusted friend and consul?" The Emperor's eyes pierced into Dar-Ota who until now had been just a bystander. Recognition of what was unfolding flashed across the face of the councillor. He knew to what the Emperor was eluding; he prayed he was wrong. He glanced at Muyda, who by now was also realising why she and Dar-Ota were there; her look of horror was not disguised. The Emperor continued "You of all people Dar-Ota, a Principal no less. Betrayal from a woman I could live with but a friend and advisor?"

"Please my Lord" yelled Muyda. "It was all my doing; I gave Principal Dar-Ota no choice…"

"Silence witch" bellowed the Emperor abruptly ending Muyda's plea.

Dar-Ota knew exactly how this would unfold. He had been around long enough. He had been an accomplished warrior for thirty years before his promotion and he wouldn't go quietly. He rammed his elbow upwards into the jaw of Cam-Sem splintering his front teeth. He spun and with all his weight behind it he hammered his fist into the nose of Zo-Sem. Both Dominators fell back, stunned by the speed and ferocity of the attack. I might be a Principal now thought Dar-Ota but I will always be a warrior. The Principal turned to Muyda. Ty-Sem had her on her knees his huge hand firmly clamped onto her shoulder and his falcata already drawn with the blade biting slightly into her neck. The Principal backed away as the two Dominators picked themselves up off the floor, Cam-Sem spitting broken teeth and blood onto the floor. The Emperor had not moved and neither had Danus Venra, although a smug smile crept across her flawless visage.

There would be no ceremony, no words and no quarter given. The world in which they lived was completely based on the principles of right and wrong, and what would seem like brutality to an outsider was simply practicality. Cam-Sem turned to the Emperor, he gave a simple nod and he turned back to face Dar-Ota. He reached behind his back with both hands and un-clicked two shiva. The shiva was an ancient weapon and consisted of a crescent shaped blade attached to a handle and a tubular brace. Cam-Sem slid his hands through the braces and curled his armoured fingers around the grips. He smiled at the Principal, his smile a mockery of broken teeth and blood.

Dar-Ota circled the Dominator. He would have relished the adrenaline of combat with one of the Emperor's Dominators, perhaps a little more if he had been armed or even armoured. As it was he was garbed only in his sleeveless white Principal's tunic, with a black stole draped around his neck, it bore the symbols of his office. He removed the stole and tied it around his waist, as the two warriors continued to circle each other. 'Speed' thought Dar-Ota, it is my only advantage. Even as the thought occurred Cam-Sem leapt forward slashing the shiva towards his throat, Dar-Ota's reactions took over and he dropped to the floor like a stone. As he did he swung his right leg out in an arc and brought it into Cam-Sem's Knee with a thunderous crack.

The Principal knew how strong the ceramic armour was, but he also knew every weak point. The Dominator toppled back like a felled tree landing with a resounding crack as his armoured back thudded into the floor, and his breath escaped him. Dar-Ota bounded over the prone form slipping his small ceremonial blade from his calf scabbard. He landed with one knee on the breastplate and one knee on the left bicep of Cam-Sem pinning it in place. He plunged the blade repeatedly into the right armpit of the pinned warrior. The knife skewered the mass of nerves and paralysed the Dominator's right side.

Dar-Ota reached down and slid the shiva off the lifeless limb and slid it over his own right hand. Cam-Sem had not given up his struggle and was frantically trying to free his left arm so he could bring it to bear on his attacker. Dar-Ota arched his back and brought the shiva down onto the elbow joint. The blade sliced through the weaker armour straps and severed the Dominator's left arm, making a final chink as it bit into the temple floor. He raised the shiva again and punched it down on the side of the neck guard. The protector popped and the piece of metal sprung clear revealing his next target. In a swift sideways movement Dar-Ota severed the jugular. Cam-Sem brought his handless limb towards his throat in a futile attempt to stem the blood. He coughed and blood erupted from the gash in his neck. Dar-Ota retrieved the severed limb and took the other shiva, he turned to face his next opponent.

Muyda watched the unfolding scene, tears in her eyes, awaiting the inevitable. Dar-Ota was a proud man and he would not go to the depths quietly, but go he would, and she would follow shortly behind him, of that she was sure.

Zo-Sem wasn't going to make the same mistake as his friend, he would not underestimate his opponent, coupled with the fact he was now armed. Zo-Sem's armour was the same as the other Dominators except that his vambraces had been modified. As he stepped forward to face Dar-Ota he clenched his fists tightly and blades as long as his forearms sprang out over his fists, turning each arm into a deadly sword. Each blade was serrated on the inner edge and the outer edge was interrupted by a hooked incision. The armour casing that held the blades now doubled as extra armour and could be used to block as well as attack.

The pair eyed each other carefully, mentally baiting the other to make the first move. Dar-Ota caved first jumping and spinning three hundred and sixty degrees lashing out his arm as he spun. Zo-Sem raised his arm to block the strike and the shiva sparked off the armour, but left no other impact. Zo-Sem retaliated in a rapid flurry of moves, slicing and jabbing. The onslaught was so quick and powerful it took every bit of skill from the Principal to block the attacks. The temple rang out with the sound of metal on metal. Zo-Sem pressed his advantage which eventually paid off as his arm blade passed the guard of Dar-Ota and penetrated his left shoulder. Zo-Sem withdrew the arm blade and stepped back from his victim.

The pain was like fire inside his shoulder, his grip deserted him and the shiva clanked to the floor. Zo-Sem renewed his attack swiping at the head of his opponent. The Principal moved back and as his did he dropped to one knee, the arm blade passed harmlessly over his head. He simultaneously rammed the remaining shiva up under Zo-Sem's kilt into his groin severing the femoral artery. Zo-Sem's arms went limp his strength draining like the blood pouring from his wound, he tried to lift his arms but Dar-Ota easily swatted them away. Mustering his strength Dar-Ota punched the shiva toward the face of his enemy. The power of the blow sliced completely through Zo-Sem's mouth almost decapitating him. His eyes rolled and his dead body crashed to the flagstones, blood from his wounds pooling on the floor.

Dar-Ota stood defiant, he looked at Muyda, and he could see the pride and love in her eyes. He was glad he had the courage to face the depths as a warrior.

Lord Senn stood up from his throne and thumped the two catches that retained his cloak. As he strode forward the white fur cloak fell to the floor behind him. He reached behind his back and brought out two metal bars. His thumbs eased a catch on top of each and the weapons sprang to life with a well oiled click. They telescopically extended to the length of an arm and then a hammer head rotated to form a right angle. At the other end of the hammer head was a long spike. These war hammers were the Emperor's weapons of choice and had served him well in many campaigns. As the Emperor approached him Dar-Ota dropped his remaining shiva. The Emperor would have to kill an unarmed man. The Emperor never even broke his stride; he unleashed a blur of hammer blows with terrifying force, each blow breaking and shattering bone.

The broken body of Principal Dar-Ota sagged to its knees as the Emperor reversed the hammer in his hand and he struck the final blow. The spike of the hammer head buried into Dar-Ota's skull up to the haft. Lord Senn released his grip on the hammer as the dead Principal fell forward, gravity pulling his face into the floor. The Emperor put his armoured foot on the head of the corpse and tugged his hammer free. He reached down and clinically wiped the cranial fluid from the spike. He stood and clicked the catches, the hammers folded and retracted and in one graceful movement were again attached to the back of his armour.

"Just get it over with you coward" snarled Muyda through gritted teeth. Her Dominator guard fiercely slapped his gauntleted hand across her face producing a large red welt across her cheek. The Emperor held up his hand and once again Ty-Sem stepped back.

"That would be too easy my dear wife" explained Senn. "I couldn't possibly have you killed for adultery. People simply wouldn't believe you could have chosen another man over me! No it's much simpler than that. I am disowning you. You will be cast down to GebShu and join the ranks of the nameless Murai. If you survive the rapists and murderers, you will continue to serve me in the granaries of Imercia."

"No, please my Lord" Muyda begged. Senn continued as if deaf to Myuda's plea.

"I shall inform the people that I grew tired of you, that you no longer satisfied the Emperor's needs." He turned away from Muyda. "And perhaps I shall take Danus Venra as my new wife." Muyda looked across at Venra; she was grinning and gave a coy wink. Muyda raised herself up, anger boiling inside which she could no longer contain.

"You can do what you like with me" she spat. "But my son will return and fulfil the prophecy. I only wish I could be here to see him cleave your head from your shoulders." The Emperor paused and turned. For the first time his calm exterior faded.

"If you truly believe one of my sons would turn on me then know that I would mutilate their bodies and send the unrecognizable crippled chunks of flesh to join you on Gebshu. Take her away" he commanded. Ty-Sem grabbed Muyda's arms as the Emperor gave his final order. "Ty-Sem, inform the clerics there are two openings in my personal bodyguard. Trials to be held on the morrow. Oh, and we have an opening for a Principal also." And with that he walked to Venra who placed her hand on his arm and they strolled away into the Sanctuary. Muyda felt hopeless as she was led away, but hope flared as she thought of the one thing that would keep her going. Her secret. Her son. The prophecy.

*

The two brothers Vas-Te and Bok-Te walked across the training ground courtyard. Vas-Te was a clear forearm's height taller and wider than his younger brother, but his size in no way hampered the bigger man. His muscled frame rippled beneath his black tunic.

"What do you reckon he wants with us?" said the smaller of the two men.

"The challenge" stated Vas-Te.

"What challenge?" Asked a surprised and intrigued Bok-Te.

21

"Two of the Emperor's Dominators were killed. There is an arena challenge event. I am guessing he wants us to enter."

"That's excellent news" exclaimed the young brother. "I have been waiting ages for a chance like this."

"You and me both brother" said the big man. Bok-Te thought for a second and asked.

"What if we get drawn against each other?"

"Then I'd have to kill you" said the big man completely serious.

"You'd have to catch me first you fat lump" and with that Bok-Te thumped his brother in the arm and ran across the courtyard to the arena. The arena was a circular amphitheatre, the central pit covered in sand and a stone pillar twice the height of a man stood in the centre. Outside the pit fifty rows of seats disappeared up into the distance. The whole arena was covered by a suspended roof with an opening in the centre, letting the light flood down in a vertical column illuminating the killing ground. In the past there had been a special area for the Emperor and his retinue, but that had long been removed and the arena was now completely symmetrical. When the Emperor attended the arena he sat with the rest of the Dumonii. It was supposed to signify his empathy and connection with the masses.

The Lord Emperor was in the central pit strolling around the arena, tracing gauges in the masonry with his fingers as if he had purposely carved them himself. Bok-Te saw the Emperor and raced towards him dropping to one knee and giving the customary forearm salute across his chest. Bok-Te, although enthusiastic, knew his place and the etiquette he should use when in the presence of the Emperor, his father.

"Good morning my Lord" greeted Bok-Te.

"No need for formalities my son. Stand and let me look at you." Bok-Te quickly rose to his feet always wanting to please. The Emperor grabbed him by the arms. Even in his most tactile moments Bok-Te could feel the power in his father's arms.

"Where is that hulk brother of yours?" asked Lord Senn.

"I am here father" shouted Vas-Te as he entered the arena. The Emperor turned to see the huge frame of his eldest son squeeze through the doorway. Vas-Te strode across the arena and imitated his brother's actions by falling to one knee and saluting.

"You know why I have brought you here" stated the Emperor.

"Yes father, the challenge" answered Vas-Te standing.

"It is time for you to take your place at my side" he said looking directly at Vas-Te.

"And me also father?" asked Bok-Te puzzled at why his father's statement had been directed at his brother.

"No my son, it is not your time. I wanted to tell you in person. Your time will come, but it is not this day." Bok-Te could feel the anger and frustration well within him; he wanted to blurt out questions, statements, and proof that he was ready. He knew better and attempted to quell the burning passion inside.

"As you wish father. I am honoured you have told me in person." His face made a poor attempt of hiding his disappointment.

"Wait outside my young son; I will speak with your brother alone." Bok-Te stood straight, bowed and saluted.

"At the Emperor's command" said Bok-Te quietly. He turned and left the arena.

"He'll get over it" said Vas-Te confidently.

"It matters not" stated the Emperor. "It is you that must tread these sands. Have you prepared?"

"There is no man amongst the Reavers or the Missionrai who can stand against me" said Vas-Te assuredly.

"Your complacency will be your undoing my son. Never underestimate your opponent. The reason we have this challenge in the first place is because an unarmed Principal bested two of my Dominators." His voice betrayed the respect he had for the recently murdered Principal Dar-Ota.

"It is as you say my Lord. I have confidence in my abilities and I will destroy whoever stands before me in this arena." Vas-Te spoke quietly with an unintentional edge to his voice but with absolute certainty of his words.

"Anything else would simply not do" smiled the Emperor as he clasped the forearms of his eldest son. Vas-Te saluted and turned to leave. As he bent over to exit the arena, he turned to his father.

"What was the real reason you didn't want Bok to fight my Lord?" The Emperor laughed as he answered.

"I wouldn't want you to kill him." Satisfied with that fact, Vas-Te left the arena to prepare.

*

Muyda had spent the night in a holding cell. She was going over and over yesterday's events in her head. She felt a terrible guilt. Had she said too much? She had wanted to hurt the Emperor, her husband, and had lashed out with her words. She was sure she hadn't given anything away. Her secret was safe, the child she had with Dar-Ota many revolutions ago was safe, she was sure. If the Emperor had expected anything she would have been interrogated. She thought about Vas-Te and Bok-Te. They only clamoured for their father's attention; they hadn't spoken to her for years. She knew the Emperor would look at them differently after her outburst about the Prophecy, but she felt no guilt at what might happen if the Emperor became too paranoid.

She was woken from her thoughts by the clanking of metal as the key entered the lock to her cell and the door was thrown open. There stood two Reavers. She didn't recognize either soldier. Muyda studied them. They were both in their late forties, probably had served in the shock troops in their early years and now had opted for the easy life of prisoner transport. The taller of the two men had a jagged scar across his cheek that continued down under his chin and across his neck. He had seen action of some sort she thought. The scarred man looked at Muyda like a man about to devour his prey. Muyda sensed the lust and stepped back against the wall.

"Don't worry my Lady" said the scarred man. "We are under strict orders that you remain..." he paused, "intact" he added. "Tis just formalities" he looked at his partner and smiled. "If you could just remove your clothes for us and put this brocard on."He tossed the brocard at Muyda's feet. Muyda stared at the brocard. It was a short sleeveless dress made from a course material. It was stained and it stank.

"It's what all the fashionable unnamed are wearing these days" chuckled the guard. "Now put it on witch." Muyda raised herself up and rallied her courage. She stared at the men and then spat onto their boots. The scarred man stepped forward and grabbed her by the hair yanking her head back; with his other hand he punched her hard in the stomach. Muyda doubled over and as she did a fist came down on the side of her head knocking her to the ground. Her head swam. She tried to roll over onto her front, but the guard had her pinned. He started tearing at her clothes like a wild animal; she could feel his coarse nails scraping against her flesh. Sweat dripped from his head onto her naked chest and she smelt the foul odour of his breath and body consume her.

"Bring it in" she heard him say. He continued to rip at her clothes and she was now lying completely naked with the guard sat astride her. The second Reaver appeared with a small brazier and took out the iron rod that protruded from it and handed it to his scarred accomplice. The brand sizzled, and she could see the glowing red numbers. The second guard knelt down with his knees either side of her head. She struggled with everything she had but the scarred man forced the brand down onto her forehead. She smelt her burning flesh and for an instant felt no pain, then it came like a flood searing through her skin. She screamed and lost consciousness.

Muyda's whole body and mind were an inferno. She opened her eyes to see the two guards staring down at her. The scarred man adjusted his belt and tunic. She heard them laughing as she felt the urine splashing onto her face and re-igniting the brand on her forehead.

"This is my special blend of antiseptic." The laughter rang in her ears and her mind retreated from her physical body.

*

The din of the arena was intense. There hadn't been a challenge match for a while let alone two at once. Nearly all seats were taken and only a few in the high reaches remained empty. The Emperor flanked by Venra, the four Virtues and the remainder of his Dominators, sat close to the edge of the pit wall and were deep in conversation.

A bellowing horn sounded and the noise of the arena stopped in an instant, replaced by eager anticipation. There was very little in the way of ceremony. The civilization had prospered on efficiency and needless words or oratory got in the way of the action and purpose of the challenge. The horn sounded twice and the single door to the arena pit opened.

Two men entered, both Missonrai. They were clad only in small kilts. Each fighter was covered in tattoos from head to toe, mostly in scripted prayers, but one of the men, Shun-Te, had the Emperor's sun motif on his back. Both men were ripped with muscle and strode into the arena like they owned it. The crowd erupted with rapturous applause and cheers. The combatants took their places at either side of the central pillar, neither fighter able to see the other. The fighters were completely unarmed but at the top of the pillar hung a vicious selection of blades and other exotic weapons.

The challenge usually went one of two ways. The fighters would battle hand to hand, or both would climb the pillar using the small holds on the pillar, grab a weapon and then fight. Both men braced themselves. The horn sounded once more to signal the start of the bout. Both men leapt forward and assailed the pillar. Shun-Te, the man with the tattooed sun on his back, dropped to the ground first clutching an enormous double headed axe in his hands. He rounded the pillar to face his opponent. To his surprise he wasn't there. He quickly looked up to see the other fighter stood aloft the pillar with a mace in one hand and kuriken in the other. The kuriken was a three bladed throwing weapon, each blade the length of a hand. The fighter launched the kuriken towards Shun-Te and as he did so he somersaulted off the pillar. Shun-Te blocked the missile by knocking it to the floor. He managed to lift the heavy axe in time to block a fierce strike from the flanged mace. Both backed away. The fight was on.

The smaller of the two men, Urun-Te, attacked first and leapt in the air swinging his mace with both hands. Shun-Te blocked the mace but as he landed the nimble Urun-Te thrust out his foot catching Shun-Te in the stomach and launching him across the pit. He landed heavily but rose quickly, sand sticking to his back like glue. Shun-Te gritted his teeth and charged. He swung the axe with one hand in a decapitating arc, but Urun-Te ducked beneath the blow and then back flipped away from the returning strike. The crowd roared, eager for first blood.

Both fighters again faced off, the bigger man now breathing heavily and sweating profusely. Again Urun-Te leapt at the big man attempting a strike to the side of his head. His attack blocked, he tried to sweep the front leg but his move was read and Shun-Te lifted his front foot to avoid the leg sweep. Urun-Te stepped back slightly off balance only to feel the foot of his opponent smash into his ribcage and send him sprawling across the pit. Shun-Te pressed his advantage and with a thunderous strike brought the axe over his head and down towards his foe. The smaller fighter blocked the blow taking the force in his arms, but the axe blade bit deep into the haft of the mace. Another strike and the mace would fold. He needed another weapon. He waited for the next strike, which was another overhead strike. He dived to the side, avoiding death by a finger. Shun-Te's axe thunked into the sand of the arena floor. Urun-Te dropped his mace and leapt for the pillar in a gamble to get a new weapon. He climbed swiftly but looked back to see the axe swinging towards his leg. He jumped for a war maul to his right and avoided the blow, but although his fingers clutched at the maul's handle he could not keep his grip. His hand slid off and he landed in the pit weapon-less.

Shun-Te withdrew his axe from the pillar; a large chunk of kullstone fell to the floor dislodged by the strike. He moved towards the crouching figure, knowing he would have to attempt to retrieve his mace. Shun-Te feigned a left thrust with his axe, at which point Urun-Te charged to the right and towards his weapon. Shun-Te reversed his body movement as planned and brought his left leg around in an arc, his heel connecting with Urun-Te's jaw. It made a hollow thud as the jaw broke. Urun-Te took one shaky step back and saw the axe lift and the blade glint in the light. He lifted his arm in a pathetic attempt to block the attack. The axe passed straight through the arm and buried itself deep into his chest cleaving the heart. For a split second there was silence, then the masses went berserk, shouting and screaming. Shun-Te walked towards the Emperor and saluted. The horn sounded once again to end the duel.

Vas-Te stared through the barred window on the pit door. A trap door opened and several men emerged to drag the dead body beneath the sands and fresh weapons were reset atop the pillar. Shun-Te approached the door and stepped inside. He was caked in sweat, sand and blood. The warriors exchanged glances but no words. The man Vas-Te was about to fight was a Reaver. He hadn't yet made squad leader, but seemed accomplished enough. He had thought he would feel at least some remorse or pity for his opponent when they met. Vas-Te felt nothing for the man; he was just another obstacle in his way. His thoughts drifted and he wondered if his father had fixed it so that he had a weaker opponent; he hoped not.

The horn sounded twice and the two warriors stepped from the door out into the light. Vas-Te arched and stretched and walked towards his starting block. The crowd started chanting.

"Vas-Te, Vas-Te, Vas-Te."

He looked every bit the perfect warrior, massive in height and muscle. Unlike the majority of soldiers who wore their hair tight cropped, Vas-Te had two streaks of longer hair either side of his head which formed small pony tails on the back of his scalp. The rest of his head was shaved short and into this were razored patterns matching the patchwork of tattoos that covered his entire body. His opponent Yan-Su had been a Reaver for many years and had been passed over for promotion to Missionrai on more than one occasion. He wasn't sure why, maybe his temper. Whatever it was he knew this was his one chance to get the promotion he deserved and make a name for himself. He was a seasoned fighter and knew his strengths and weaknesses. He was glad when he had been drawn against Vas-Te. Taking down this popular man would increase his standing no end. As he walked to his starting block he looked across the pit at the big man. 'He won't know what hit him' he thought.

The Horn blurted, the bout was on. Yan-Su's strategy was a simple tried and tested one. Get to the pillar, grab a weapon, and then use it on his opponent before he had a chance to retrieve a weapon of his own. It had worked before.

The instant the horn had sounded, Vas-Te had sprinted forward and around the pillar, for a man of his size he moved at an incredible speed. Yan-Su had reached the column and had started to climb. As Vas-Te rounded the pillar he launched himself like a battering ram, leading with his knee into the startled body of the climber. The speed of the blow alone would have done serious damage. That coupled with the weight behind the attack cracked the ribs of Yan-Su and sent him skittering onto the floor. Landing on one foot and then launching himself again, Vas-Te plummeted towards his prone victim, this time with his other knee. It was like a comet hitting the surface of a planet, completely inescapable.

The bulk of the big Missionrai smashed the ribcage. The ribs shattered and splintered piercing the internal organs. The stricken soldier coughed blood and winced at the pain in his chest. Vas-Te rose and turned; he steadily climbed the pillar and then jumped back down to the pit holding a two handed war maul. The weapon was so heavy it could only be wielded by a man of Vas-Te's physique. He walked calmly back to where his victim was trying to sit up. Without hesitation he raised the maul over his head and brought it down in a thunderous crack. The force of the blow obliterated the skull and anything remaining of the ribcage. Even the most bloodthirsty of spectators winced at the strike. There was total silence. The bout was over in less than twenty seconds.

Vas-Te turned and held the hammer aloft with one hand and punched it into the air. The crowd erupting in applause and shouts, his name echoing around the arena. The Emperor looked on smiling, his mind planning and scheming. Venra turned to the Emperor,

"He's very impressive" she enquired. 'Maybe too much so' thought the Emperor, 'maybe that witch was right about him after all'.

*

Muyda was curled up in the foetal position hugging the corner of her cell. The physical pain was receding but the mental pain still lingered. She had traced the brand on her forehead with her fingers revealing it to be the number seventy-four. This was now how she would be known.

She heard keys rattling outside her door and she attempted to make herself smaller. The door opened and a Reaver stepped into the cell. She could tell by the wave symbol on his shoulder guard he was based on the planet Geb-Shu. She looked up into his eyes, and like all the rest she had encountered, saw no emotion.

"Stand up Murai" he barked. "Time to find you a new home."

As she walked past the soldier, he took her hands and jerked them around her back clamping on a restraining cuff which held her arms firmly behind her back. Outside of her cell were three other women all in restraints, and all looking like they had undergone a similar treatment. She filed into line and then the sorry group proceeded out through the holding cells.

"Wait there" commanded a second Reaver bringing up the rear of the group. They had stopped outside a cell door which the first guard was opening. He stepped inside.

"Get up fish boy" the guard shouted. Muyda turned to look at the woman behind her. She shrugged her shoulders, so Muyda turned back to see what was happening. Out from the cell ducked an incredibly tall but very skinny man. He was unlike anything she had seen before. He stood a great deal taller than the guard who was clacking wrist restraints on him. He wore a male brocard, which was effectively a long skirt, although on this man it only came down to his knees. His skin was darker than normal and it was covered in a striking pattern. The pattern consisted of green and blue stripes over his arms, shoulders, legs and face resembling a form of camouflage. Muyda wasn't sure if they were painted on or actually his natural skin. His hair was long and matted hanging all the way down his back, and tied within it were various shells and beads. He turned to look at the line of women, his unusual appearance punctuated by cloudy white eyes. He too filed into line and they continued out of the cells. Muyda had known their destination as she had been there before, but not like this. They headed toward the 'Gate'.

The 'Gate' was the portal that the Domonii used to travel from their satellite of Son-GebShu to the ocean planet below. She had no idea of how it worked, only that depending on which side you entered it decided where you came out. She had been thankful in the past for Gate travel as ninety percent of the food and resources used by the Dumonii came through the portal, plundered from the planet below. According to Dar-Ota there had once been hundreds of them. This was the only one she was aware of still in use. They entered the Gate chamber. The room was triangular which reflected the lines of the 3 stone pillars arranged in an equilateral triangle in the centre of the chamber. The roof above was open to the sky. The three circular pillars were almost identical, only the carved symbols distinguishing them apart. The pillars consisted of black kullstone cylinders stacked one on top of the other, spaced apart by a smaller diameter cylinder. Through the centre of all of the stones was a cylinder of pure crystal. This was Lexan stone. By each pillar stood a hunched, hooded servillisor.

"Open the gate" commanded the lead Reaver. Each servillisor began to hum, each one at a different pitch. As they continued their bizarre song the Lexan stone began to vibrate. The whole chamber then started to vibrate. Electrical sparks started to dance around the pillars. The servillisors continued their audio prayers and the electric tendrils grew until they reached out for each other. As they touched a loud 'whump' filled the chamber. Muyda could feel the gravitation pull towards the now shimmering centre of the three pillars. Holding onto the tall prisoner the Reaver stepped into the void. Muyda had always been terrified by this bit but knew it was harmless; she followed her eyes tight shut. She kept walking and then thudded into the back of a body in front of her. It was the tall prisoner. They had passed through the gate and she had felt nothing.

There were a lot more Reavers here than she had expected. Several approached the line with black cloth in their hands. A Reaver reached up and tied the cloth tightly around her eyes. They were led away and as they walked she heard the crackle and fizz of the Gate closing.

Muyda had known of the Nameless peoples, the Murai. She knew they lived here on the island of Imercia. She also knew they farmed the food for the people of Son GebShu. What she didn't know was how they lived and she wasn't prepared for what she saw before her.

The rain was falling hard which added to the miserable scene. A long main track ran down the hill to a jetty that reached out into the ocean. The water stretched out disappearing into the gloom. The track was deep in mud and sewage. On either side of the track, spreading out across the land like a sore were hundreds of shacks. There wasn't a straight line anywhere. Some shacks seemed to be built on top of others; some seemed barely big enough to accommodate a person. They looked fragile and she was convinced a fierce storm would wipe them all away. They were built from driftwood and anything else that had been discarded. Dim lights flickered from makeshift windows and doorways and smoke filtered up through the rain. The sally port of the fortress closed behind them. Muyda rubbed her wrists and looked at the others. Already cold and shivering they had started to wander into the junk town. The tall prisoner was missing.

"Where did the tall man go?" Muyda asked after the other women. One turned.

"They don't let his sort roam free outside, they keep them in the fortress" she replied.

"His sort?" questioned Muyda. The woman kept walking without answering. "Please!" she shouted a touch of desperation in her voice. "What do we do now?" The woman ahead stopped again and without turning she said,

"Find a place to live before it gets too dark."

Chapter 2 – The Hunt

The marine pods clung to the slopes of the submerged mountain like the crustaceans they supported in return. The pods stretched around the underwater mountain and down onto the slopes with a few dotted on isolated rock outcrops on the plateau floor. The community of Antykia was the last in a line of settlements which followed the Booma Mountain Range. The peoples that lived there were known as 'Enki'.

The pods were built on many stone stilts supporting a low circular stone wall. On top of the wall were huge curved bones which formed a domed framework. The skeletal frame was coated in scales each the size of a man's head. Some were highly polished becoming semi-transparent and letting light flood into the interior. At the apex of the roof a 'breathing stone' was inset. It was a living coral stone which effectively scrubbed the carbon dioxide from within the pod and released it into the ocean. On the older pods these breathing stones had grown and spread out covering most of the roof area. The ocean tribes had long since learnt to live in harmony with their watery environment and in turn Povian, God of the Sea, had provided for them. The whole pod structure was held together by a waterproof substance known as 'Rubb'. The base for the mixture was found in pools out on the plateau floor. It had a thick viscous consistency and when mixed with crushed shell reacted to form a hardened watertight bond.

The pods had been constructed on any area large enough to support the circular base, but over time connecting tubes to other pods had been added so that a single habitation now consisted of several domed pods all connected at varying levels and of varying sizes. They were covered in the sea life which covered everything else in the rocky seascape. The organic growth softened any edges and blurred the man-made structures into the living background. Bubbles from Velp fields and breathing stones were the only signal betraying the ocean tribe's presence in this underwater world.

It was early morning and Var stirred from a deep sleep. Without opening his eyes he was aware that he was being watched. He opened one eye cautiously. Already awake and sat cross legged by the side of his bed were his two younger brothers Mort and Mido. Var sighed and closed his eye.

"Come on get up, it's hunt day" chirped his brothers in unison. Var Grumbled. The two brothers jumped onto Var's bed and started shaking him. With sleepy reluctance Var sat up. He looked sternly at his two brothers; they were far too excited for this time of morning he thought, but inside he too felt a pang of adrenaline kick start his system. He grabbed each brother around the neck and brought them together in a playful hug. Each brother twisted and squirmed, and with practised ease broke free of Var's grip, then grabbing an arm each they twisted his hands back towards him locking his arms by his sides. They waited smiling in anticipation.

"Do you give in?" asked Mido.

"I suppose so" laboured Var. With that he flexed his muscles and lifted his arms sending the two boys bouncing across his bed giggling uncontrollably.

Var surveyed his room. It was only just big enough to house his bed and the white bones that arced overhead only allowed him to stand straight in the centre. He sat on the edge of his bed and pulled on his snug fitting 'skin'. The 'skin' like most of the Enki tribe was made from Sibalen hides. It was extremely flexible and provided great insulation. The 'skin' consisted of an all in one shorts and tunic combination. The black hide had faded slightly with time and wear and there were blue and green jagged stripes painted across it which matched the tattoos on his arms and legs. The shoulders of his 'skin' were made from individually stitched scales that gave much greater movement when swimming. His mother Muadin was a skilled seamstress and had made the garment after his previous one had been shredded in a Baraq attack. He touched his fingers to his stomach. The events of that day still lingered in his memory as did the angry scars than ran across his torso.

He had remembered his excitement at putting on the new 'skin' and flexing his shoulders and watching the pearlescent shimmer of light ripple across the scales. Now as he fastened the collar around his neck if felt like he had always worn it, an extension of his own skin. He fastened a knife around each shin and a belt with numerous pouches around his waist and looked into a small pearl shell at his reflection. His bright blue eyes shone back. Although he was happy with what he saw, his unique appearance had been a burden as well as a blessing. Var stood apart from the rest the tribe as he did not have the cloudy white eye membrane that protected the inner eye from saltwater. Var's father had made him a pair of polished eye shields when he was younger which had made for an interesting time at school with the other 'normal' children. The ones he wore now were streamlined, fitted to the contours of his eye sockets and tapering back behind his ears and fixed via an expanding band behind his head. The lenses were a reflective golden yellow, which Var's father had found in the nearby Ancient ruin of Coba. They were eons old, yet despite their great age they enhanced the contrast of the underwater world giving him a sharp singular view on his surroundings. Var liked them; he liked his uniqueness. It was only his friend Astur that still took any notice of them. He lifted a beaded cord from a hook on the wall and tied his long blonde hair into a single pony tail. He grabbed his flippers and harpoon and ducked through the connecting tunnel into the main pod.

Astur sat cross legged at the low table; his mother Almay and his sister Bronsur sat alongside him. Astur wore a similar skin to the rest of the tribesmen, short legged and short sleeved, but his differed slightly in colour. The main body had been painted in a deep red. It was still intersected by camouflaged stripes, but the red colour indicated that its wearer was a tribal Outrider.

The hierarchy of the Enki tribe was simple. The tribe was led by the Helmsman and supported by Tribal Anchors. Astur's father had been a Tribal Anchor for many seasons and had been on the council that had decided Astur was a suitable candidate for a Tribal Outrider. This small group were the guardians of the tribe. They kept the peace and protected the people from other tribes and the creatures from the deep that occasionally ventured close. The rest of the population worked together in family groups collecting food, building and collaborating for the greater good of the tribe. It had been this way for as long as the Wordkeeper had recorded time. There were other ocean tribes, but in the vastness of the ocean they rarely met.

Astur's sister was gently combing oil into her long dark hair. Her milky white eyes mirrored the complexion of her skin. Unlike most tribeswomen Bronsur had very little pigment in her skin and her pale skin stood in stark contrast to her ebony hair, accentuated by tiny brown pigment spots across her face and neck. The harsh contrast of colours only added to her transcendent beauty.

"Can you not do that while I'm eating?" asked Astur "I keep getting hair in my food."

"I doubt that very much" interjected his mother. "The speed you eat your food you wouldn't notice a slugvert crawling in it." Astur glared at his sister who forced a false smile and then stuck her tongue out. Astur smiled. No matter how annoying his sister was he loved her deeply. His mother looked up again from her stitching.

"Make sure you have enough beacons today. You don't want to lose anyone" she nagged.

"We'll take plenty" countered Astur.

"You know what happened last season. That poor boy that got lost; it was moons before you found him ⌐ almost out of air" she continued.

"He was fine mother, and it was only a morning, not moons he was missing" replied Astur.

"Well" his mother went on. "Gednu's boys will be there for the first time this season, and you'll need to look out to them."

"Var will be there mother" interrupted Bronsur. "I am sure he will be keeping an eye on them."

"Don't worry mother" said Astur with a long sigh. "I will be keeping an eye on everyone." Astur's mother reached across the table and placed her hand on his arm.

"I know you will dear" she said lovingly. "But most of all take care of yourself." Astur smiled at his mother, stuck his tongue out at his sister and stood to collect his things.

As Var entered the main pod Mort and Mido were busy devouring their breakfast. His mother Muadin was crouched next to the flameless stove prodding the fish which were crackling in the skillet. She looked up as Var entered.

"Yours and your father's breakfast will be ready in two shakes" she stated. Var stepped over Mido and sat down next to his father.

"Morning father" he greeted.

"Morning my boy" replied his father not looking up from the task in which he was engrossed.

"He has re-packed yours and your brother's lungs" interrupted his mother. Gednu looked up and raised his eyebrows at Var.

"Just mine left" he said with a smile and returned to the job in hand. The bio-lung was simply a container. It consisted of two canisters strapped side by side with a long tube protruding from the top of each one which met again at a mouthpiece. The bio-lung was worn on the back and the pipes passed over the shoulders to the mouthpiece. The miracle of survival beneath the waves was solely due to the green plant packed within the containers. The plant known as Velpaynix or 'Velp' took oxygen directly from the water and converted it into pure oxygen. The tribes had long since grown and harvested this precious essential crop to provide air for the pods and for the personal breathing apparatus. The Velp was packed tightly into the canisters and then filled with sea water. The plant would continue to produce oxygen for three or more moons. Var's father was using a small ramming tool to tightly pack the plant into a standalone mouthpiece unit. This was an emergency device that would provide a few extra moments of air in case anything happened to the main tanks. It was a real skill to pack the canisters tightly giving the maximum duration of breathing time. Gednu was a past master. He screwed on the end of the mouthpiece and placed it with great satisfaction on the table.

"All done" he said triumphantly. Var had been packing his own lung for many seasons but he was grateful that his father had done his this morning. Despite the exuberance of youth he could not yet match his father's skill. Besides it had become a bit of a tradition in their pod at when the hunt came around. Var's mother turned from the stove and placed a delicious red fish in front of Var and his father; she turned and busily fussed around Mort and Mido. The twins were only twelve seasons a few moons ago, but were now eligible to attend the hunt. Var thought they seemed too young; he was sure he was older when he first went on a hunt. He turned to his father.

"Was I twelve seasons on my first hunt?" he asked.

"You were indeed" answered Gednu.

"I don't really remember it" said Var.

"That's probably because you jumped out of your skin when a tiny Sibalen popped its head out of a crevice. I think you almost lost your water" laughed Gednu. The twins and Var's mother joined in the laughter. Var smiled and looked directly at his two brothers.

"At least I don't lose my water while I sleep in my bed." He turned to his father. "Or lose my water when I am late in for supper." The laughter rang out through the pod.

They donned their bio-lungs and attached two beacon sticks to each backpack. Var and his father each carried a harpoon. The harpoons had a hollow bone handle, the length of a leg and inside this slid a metal stave with a razor sharp point and barb. The metal insert could be extended by twisting the end of the bone handle. The action then released the spring loaded barb out to its full length. Var lifted his eye shields from his forehead and pushed them into place over his eyes. Gednu checked each of his son's packs before Var returned the favour and checked his. With the pre-water ritual complete and a farewell wave to Muadin, the family jumped into the plunge pool and out into the ocean.

The group swam down through the maze of pods to where the mountain flattened out. These were the oldest pods in Antykia and in the centre of them was the nest. The nest was the largest structure in the community. It was used as a meeting house, a place where the tribe would discuss everything that affected their way of life; it was used as a school and a hospital. Today it was the starting point for the hunt. All men aged twelve seasons were allowed to attend the hunt. Most men did; there were a few that abstained mainly because they were too frail or sick. It was a tradition that was not to be missed. The tribes were superstitious people and took great care not to anger their god Povian by taking too much from the ocean. They restricted their hunting of sea titans to just once every season and then each trip into the deep ocean would be in a different direction hoping not to plunder a single species.

Var followed his father up into the plunge pool of the nest. Mort and Mido were already out and waiting impatiently for their older brother and father. Var climbed from the pool and removed his breather and eye-shields. The nest was packed, a tumultuous throng of noise as neighbours, friends and families exchanged greetings and chatted fervently about the forthcoming events. Var felt a firm slap on his shoulder and turned to see his friend Astur.

"How goes it blue eyes?" said Astur cheerfully. Var had long since given up worrying about Astur's visual jibes. He meant nothing by it. It was just his way.

"I am looking forward to this" said Var, gesturing to the gathered throng. "Do you know which way we are headed, or what we are after?"

"Not sure" said Astur slowly "Father says maybe out towards Curia, but he's not sure either. The Helmsman is keeping it all a bit secretive this season." As he said this Jotnar the Helmsman appeared in the plunge pool.

He steadily climbed from the ocean, his old limbs much more at home supported by the water than out in the air. His white hair was still a thick mane that trailed down his back. His wrinkled features matched his skin giving him a slightly deflated look. Behind him came another figure, late in seasons, but still fit and active. The hubbub of the nest stopped as the second man raised himself to his full height like there had been an off switch. The man had similar skin and equipment and carried a strange looking tubular device in his hands, but the reason for the silence was his tattoos. They were black and white stripes clearly identifying him as a different tribe. Var had heard of the different ocean tribes but never seen one in the flesh. Jotnar tapped the base of his harpoon onto the floor and the clack echoed around the dome.

"Welcome my friends. Another hunt is upon us once again. It is good to see so many familiar faces and I welcome the podlings who join us for the first time." His voice was slightly croaky but he still spoke with a composed authority. "We are honoured to be joined by a brother from across the Great Rift; men of the Enki please let me introduce you to Rickron Son-Hengist Bay-Eburus." The Helmsman used the tribesman's full title which was appropriate for a formal introduction. The fact he was

'Bay-Eburus' meant he was part of the Eburus tribe. This had caused a gasp from the elder tribesmen present. They knew that this man must have travelled across the Great Rift to be here, and that was impossible. Jotnar continued his address.

"Gentlemen, please show your appreciation for our honoured guest." The gathered crowd all tapped their harpoons onto the floor creating a loud thwack which rebounded around the chamber. "Today my friends we will travel into the deep southern ocean to hunt a Murmur," announced Jotnar. There had been shock before at the sight of Rickron, but now the tribesmen were stunned into silence. Var looked at this father who was staring open mouthed at the elderly leader. Jotnar smiled at the reaction his words had caused. "Our guest has explained to me how they hunt these great leviathans in his tribe. I am confident we can learn from him and make this a successful hunt for the people of the Enki." For the first time Var had trouble swallowing the words of the Helmsman. They were Enki. They should do things their way, not follow some stranger on a fool's crusade for a mythical creature. Jotnar cleared his throat.

"My Brothers." He held his hand aloft. "Let us pray." All present dropped to their knees and bowed their heads slightly. "Great Lord of the ocean, grant us favour this moon, and allow us a token of your bounty, so that we may continue our lives in your service. We ask that your guiding light looks over us and will return us safely to the nest of our birth. Great Povian protect us." The gathered congregation repeated in a low harmony.

"Povian protect us."

As they stood to gather their things, Jotnar hammered the floor with his harpoon once more.

"Please ensure all families take extra beacons as you leave." He gestured towards a large pile of spare beacons. Var looked at his father for reassurance, but he saw none.

*

The column of bodies swam in a long line South from the mountains. At the front was Jotnar accompanied by Rickron. The remainder of the tribe followed behind with the Tribal Outriders flanking the line on either side. Gednu, Var and the twins were close to the rear. As they reached the outer reaches Jotnar signalled to the lead swimmer. The man grabbed a beacon stick and firmly planted it into the seabed. The beacon stick was simply a long piece of bone with a spool of rope at one end, and a brightly coloured shell above it. The man grabbed the end of the rope and continued to swim onwards. When the rope had fully unwound he took a second stick and planted this into the sand, attaching the first piece of rope to it. He then swam on again repeating the process. In this way the tribe would take it in turns to plant the lifeline that would guide them back to safety. There was no other way of navigating beneath the waves. The similar surroundings all faded into the distance even in good visibility, but strong underwater currents and even some of the big creatures could stir up the sand and silt making it difficult to see your hand in front of your face.

Var's mind was swimming along with his body. He was excited at the thought of hunting a Murmur if they did actually exist, but at the same time Rickron bothered him. He was obviously from another tribe, his tattoos proved it, but Eburus? There was no way he had swum across the Great Rift. The Great Rift or Black River ran as far as the tribes could tell all the way around the world. It was a massive chasm. It had no bottom and no end. Through it ran a powerful current that could drag anything or anyone foolish enough to get too close.

They had been swimming for some time and Var and his family were nearing the front of the lifeline. Var had clicked his flippers together and was using both legs in unison. It helped to vary the pattern of kicks so as not to fatigue his muscles. He un-clicked them and twisted over onto his back to face his father behind, He used his free hand to signal in sign language to his father.

<<Soon>>

His father nodded and signed back.

<<Alert>>

Var sensed it too. Something was wrong. Var looked out into the distance his lenses giving him a crisp view of the underwater scene. There were several rock outcrops covered in coral up ahead teaming with fish and something larger in the distance moving way off to the left. Suddenly one of the Outriders came swimming in at speed signalling to Jotnar.

<<Tracks>>

The Helmsman called a halt to the procession and he and Rickron followed the Outrider to view his find. They Signalled.

<<Follow>>

As Var swam up to the 'track' he could not understand what he was seeing. There was a deep gauge in the seabed about waist deep and the width of two men. It continued for about a spool to the South where it seemed to be interrupted and then continued on again into the gloom. Either side of the strange trench the rock and sand had been disturbed. Jotnar signalled to the lead swimmer.

<<No Beacons>>

They swam along the great trench. Another bad omen thought Var; even though there was a huge gash in the seabed to follow we should still be using the beacon sticks. Then he stopped suddenly as if stung, his sharp vision picking out the detail before the others around him had seen anything. It had to be a Murmur.

The Murmur was an anomaly among the leviathans of the deep. It was so massive it could never have survived out of the water, but it looked completely out of place where it was. It had no fins or tail. It walked on four massive legs across the sea floor. It had a stubby head with bone protrusions and hard scales all around the top of its back and legs. It had a squat tail which seemed to serve no other purpose than balance. Underneath its armoured head was a huge jaw. The Murmur could lower its front legs dropping its gargantuan mouth into the sand. It would drive itself forward with its powerful legs excavating a huge trench as it went. It devoured anything that it captured in its trawl of the sea floor.

As they swam closer, the sheer enormity of it seemed overpowering. The long line had dissipated and spread out only a few lengths from the Murmur. All were motionless completely awestruck. The behemoth lowered its jaw and slowly shunted its way through the silt. Var turned to look at his father.

<<How Kill?>>

He signed. His father shrugged. The Murmur was at least the height of six men and twice as long. Even a sharp harpoon would not pierce its bony armature. The only target would be the underbelly. Var looked back at the giant creature. It lifted its head and shook it from side to side spilling huge amounts of sand into the ocean obscuring it from view. It was not bothered by the presence of man. The Murmur had no predators.

Var looked at Jotnar. He, like the rest of the tribe, was still staring at the majesty of the sea giant. Rickron was nowhere to be seen. Var scanned the seascape. He couldn't see any sign of the outsider, but back to his right he could see something. He tapped his father on the shoulder and signalled to him and the twins.

<<Follow>>

They swam away from the tribe over a coral outcrop. Further out beyond they could all now see what Var had spotted. It was a huge red cloud drifting slowly, tendrils outstretched through the water. As the sea currents moved the red cloud towards the tribe, it cleared a small patch close to the watching family. Through the red mist they could make a large chunk of flesh tethered to a buoy waist high from the sea floor. It was this and many more like it that were oozing blood into the water.

<<Blood!>>

Gednu signalled to Var. The horror of what was before them was all too clear. Var crouched down and his brothers and father followed suit.

<<Trap>>

He signalled.

<<Warn Others>>

Before the family could do anything about the situation the reason for the bait cloud became apparent. From out of the blood red sea a huge black shape appeared. A Baraq thought Var and shuddered at the memory. It wasn't a Baraq; it was much worse. The immense black shape came into focus as it cleared the blood haze. It was a Mammon.

The Mammon was the second largest animal in the ocean, second only to the docile Murmur. Although not the largest it was certainly the most deadliest. It had a tapered but slightly snub nose, with black eyes set atop its snout. It had a huge jaw with row upon row of serrated razor sharp teeth. Around its head it had a thick bone carapace. The bone armour was segmented and ran down the length of its tapered body ending in a huge V shaped fin. It had two seams of bony fins running down the length of its back and powered itself through the water with two massive flippers. As well as its sheer bulk and razored maw it had a unique attribute. Around the bony carapace that surrounded its head like a thick scarf were a series of holes. In these holes the creature secreted cartilage to make its own bony spears which it could eject into the water at terrifying pressure.

The leviathan was very fast for such a massive creature. It opened its mouth and swooped on the unsuspecting tribe. A few of them turned at the last minute only to scream in silence as they were sucked into the giant mouth. The Mammon snapped its jaws shut, severing bodies. Lifeless limbs and torsos floated down from the giant's mouth. As it swam on its great tail mixing the chunks of body parts with the panicking tribesmen into a ghoulish soup of blood and bubbles.

Var was shaken from his nightmare vision by his father. He turned and focused.

<<Lifeline>>

Signalled Var to his father.

<<Swim Fast>>

He signalled to his terrified brothers. They nodded and started swimming back towards the Murmur trench. When Var saw they were on their way, he turned back. He wouldn't leave the rest of his tribe behind. As he returned to the scene of the massacre the huge fish had turned and was now heading back for its second course. The tribesmen were now rallying and had extended their harpoons ready for a strike. As the Mammon approached it flexed its gills seeming to take a deep breath and then spewed the bony spears into the water. The jagged bony steaks skewered the hapless tribesmen. Some screamed letting go of their mouthpieces, instantly filling their lungs with seawater. Perhaps a small blessing as the giant jaws closed again on the dead and dying. The Mammon swam on, a handful of harpoons protruding from its underbelly.

Var twisted his harpoon and the barbed point shot out. He swam fast and saw Astur and several other Outriders. He made it to them in a couple of kicks. He stopped and signalled.

<<Cover>>

The remaining Enki were swimming for their lives back
down towards the trench. Var, Astur and half a dozen
others swam desperately for the cover of the coral
outcrop. They reached it and ducked into any available
crevice. They looked back. The Mammon had circled
round and was now coming up the Murmur's trench.
With a yet un-satiated blood thirst, it devoured the fleeing
men and swam on swallowing its prey as it approached.

As the shadow of the immense beast flooded over the
cowering survivors, Var wrapped the leather thong on his
harpoon around his wrist. As the Mammon loomed over
their hiding place the remaining Enki rammed their
harpoons into the soft belly of the creature. Var did the
same. The creature felt the stings from the harpoons and
kicked its tail to escape the feeling. As it did it wrenched
Var from the rocks by his wrist and he trailed behind the
sea monster. He reached out for one of the other
harpoons jutting from the creatures flesh. He grabbed one
and tore it free, the barb slicing through the blubber. The
Mammon twisted and turned still trying to shake the
stinging pain. The pressure on Var's wrist was intense, but
he bit down on his mouthpiece and plunged the harpoon
into the animal all the way to the handle. He dragged it
free and repeated the process. In a killing frenzy he
stabbed and stabbed, opening up a huge wound. He raised
the bloody spear again but as he did the harpoon holding
him to the creature in their death bond, split through the

skin and released him tumbling over and over in the wake of the injured monster. As one last act of unintentional defiance the huge tail thwated Var as it propelled itself away to the depths. The blow thudded into Var's back smashing one bio-lung and cracking the other.

*

Back at the coral island Astur was in the same position as he had been when he first crested the small rock outcrop. As he had rounded the rock a glittering blade had been thrust at his neck and his arms had been pinned fast. He had remained pinned as the Mammon had passed overhead and his friends had thrown their harpoons. Astur looked up to see Rickron and twenty or more Eburus warriors. They had the remaining Enki tribesmen held with knives or harpoons at their throats. To Astur's horror one of them was his father.

Rickron was still holding the strange tube he had when he had arrived back at the nest. He reached into it and removed what looked like a translucent cloth. He opened it up. It was made of many curved segments forming a crude domed bag. He then strangely put the bag over his head. He turned the tube upside down and moved it up into the bag. He reached inside and opened a valve. Air erupted from the tube filling the dome with air. When the canister had emptied Rickron stood with his head and shoulders in the air pocket. He removed his mouthpiece. Astur was forced forward and up into the temporary air bubble. The Eburus guard holding his arms ripped out his mouthpiece. He was staring at Rickron a few hands length from his face.

"We don't have much time, so just to show you I mean business," He turned to one of his men and nodded. The guard holding the Enki tribesman plunged his knife into the neck of the helpless man and brought it out forwards in a sawing motion cutting through his windpipe. The dying man clasped both hands around his throat as the air of life escaped through his fingers.

"You bastard" snarled Astur. Rickron turned and nodded again. The next guard along repeated the murderous actions of his comrade. Astur's father was next in line. "Ok, ok, what do you want?" sobbed Astur.

"Listen and listen carefully" said Rickron. "In two moons time head west from your pods and beacon a line to the edge of the black river. Do it alone" he ordered. "Do this one thing and I will return these men unharmed. Do anything else, or tell anyone else, I will feed them to the Kekken and descend upon your pods and kill everything that breathes air." Astur could not believe what was happening. "Are we clear?" shouted Rickron, the water starting to reach his chin.

"Yes" moaned Astur. The mouthpiece was forced back into his mouth and once again he faced Rickron with sea water between them. He chanced a glance at his father and then back at Rickron.

<<Go>>

Rickron signalled. Astur turned and swam for the lifeline. When he was out of sight Rickron turned to his warriors and wiped his thumb across his throat.

Var was dazed. He was lying on his back. Povian was with him; his breather was still in place. He saw the stream of bubbles escaping over his shoulder and new it was bad news. He removed his bio-lung and saw that one cylinder was completely smashed and the other cracked and unusable also. He was at least three hundred spools from home; his emergency breather wouldn't be enough on its own. He would have to swim fast. He thanked the gods that his father had packed it this morning; that was sure to give him extra time.

He looked around scared that the murderous Mammon would re-appear, but there was nothing. He had travelled several spools attached to the creature and he squinted trying to find his way back. Out in the murky distance he could see a column of bubbles. He set off immediately both fins clicking together as he shot through the water. He arrived at the grisly scene and struggled to keep the contents of his stomach on the inside. He turned one body and started back as he recognized Astur's father. He removed the bio-lung from the dead man and strapped it on. He looked at the other bodies, small creatures already starting to reclaim them. There was no Astur. His thoughts turned to his father and brothers. He kicked his flippers and powered towards home.

Chapter 3 – The Kekken

Vas-Sem, as he was now known after his promotion to Dominator, fastened his ceramic armour and clicked his cloak onto the shoulder epaulets. Ty-Sem stood waiting for him to get ready.

"Come on hurry it up. It's best not to keep him waiting even if he is your father" He said sarcastically. The massive figure of Vas-Sem slowly turned his head.

"I know my place. Make sure you know yours" he said sternly. Ty-Sem held the bigger mans gaze. There was no give in either man. Ty-Sem turned to leave.

"I'll tell the Lord Emperor you're just having a few difficulties dressing yourself." Ty-Sem smiled to himself as he strode off towards the sanctuary. Vas-Sem smiled also. He respected Ty-Sem even if he was a tedious bore. He clacked the last cloak catch into place and hurried after his comrade.

The two Dominators entered the sanctuary shoulder to shoulder, both trying their utmost not to look like they were racing each other, but neither wanting to fall behind. In the centre of the sanctuary was the Lord Emperor and sitting slightly beneath him was Jinn-Aka, Virtue of Water. The sanctuary was an inner courtyard of the great temple. It was open to the sky and consisted of ever decreasing and descending circular stone steps, which led down to a central pool of water. Standing proudly in the centre of the pool there grew an ancient sepal tree. The tree was said to have been planted by the first God Emperor when he first visited Son-Gebshu. The vast canopy now shaded the sanctuary from Shu's harsh rays and provided shelter for the current Lord Emperor and his retinue, to meet and discuss affairs of the state. Its gnarled trunk and twisted and deformed branches betrayed its old age. The majestic tree had seen and heard the history of Son-Gebshu unfold in the eons it had stood as a passive bystander as the people it guarded issued their commands. It seemed sad that such a place of beauty and serenity was the birthplace of destruction, war and deceit.

The Emperor looked up as the two men approached. Both dropped to one knee and saluted in synchronized perfection. The Emperor stood.

"These are two of my most trusted men, Ty-Sem and Vas-Sem." The two Dominators stood and bowed politely in the direction of Lord Senn's Guest.

"I am honoured to meet you both. I am Jinn-Aka the Virtue of Water." All four men sat on the stone steps. The surface of Son-Gebshu was divided into five districts. The central district surrounding the capital Sagen-Ita and the Sea of Serenity were known as the Sacred Kingdom of Rebirth, ruled directly by Lord Senn and his council. The other four areas were known as the four virtues. The virtues of fire, earth, air and water. The Lord Emperor delegated control of these districts and the leader of each took on the title of virtue.

Jinn-Aka had been the Virtue of Water for more than twenty revolutions. He was older than the other men present as his weathered skin bore testament. He was smaller in height than most Dumonii and although slight in build he was well muscled for a man of his age. He had short cropped hair which was white and running through it was a singular red stripe. He had tattoos running up his throat and onto his chin which at first glance looked like a beard. All of these attributes made for a striking appearance and underpinning this visage were his eyes. Like most of the warrior race he had eye implants that provided protection from Shu's rays, but unlike the majority his were blood red.

"The Virtue has given me some disheartening news" Lord Senn started, looking directly at the two Dominators. He turned and gestured at Jinn-Aka "Pray continue your report." The enigmatic figure of Jinn-Aka stood, straightened his robes and cleared his throat.

"In the deep southern desert there is a small outpost called Ortha-Hab. I am not sure whether you are familiar with it?" questioned Jinn-Aka. The two men shook their heads. "Well anyway," continued the Virtue. "The Missionrai in charge did not manage to send in his tribute at the last thanksgiving. I thought this slightly strange as the outlying settlements like to do things their own way, and not paying the tribute will mean the eyes of the Emperor will focus upon them." He looked at the Emperor. "Please forgive me for my bluntness my Lord."

The Emperor waved him to continue. "So I sent one of my councillors. After four turns had passed there was still no sign of my envoy."

"Have you sent in the Reavers?" interrupted Vas-Sem.

"Indeed I have" answered Jinn-Aka. "They too have not returned." There was a silent pause as they digested the information.

"How long has it been since you sent in the Reavers?" asked Lord Senn.

"Three turns" replied the Virtue. "I would have come to you sooner my Lord...."

"Nonsense" blurted the Emperor. "Your timing is not an issue here my friend." Vas-Sem could see Jinn-Aka physically relax.

"How many Reavers did you send?" added Vas-Sem.

"I sent a single grounder with a crew of five. I thought this would be plenty," stated Jinn-Aka.

"I agree a grounder with five men would be more than enough for a desert outpost, whatever trouble awaited them" said a confident and confused Ty-Sem.

"It appears not" said the Emperor standing. "Where is your young brother?" said the Emperor addressing his eldest son.

"He is on Imercia I believe my Lord" replied Vas-Sem.

"Go and fetch him and his squad of Reavers. They have experience of the desert and mountain regions. Ty-Sem will accompany you also. Go to...." The Emperor paused. "Where is the nearest gate?"

"Morlok-Tun my Lord" answered Jinn-Aka immediately.

"You will take the squad to Morlok-Tun, take a grounder and find out what is going on. You will do whatever is required to get to bottom of this" ordered Lord Senn.

"Yes my Lord" the two Dominators answered in unison, then they both turned to scowl at the other.

"I am grateful for your swift action my Lord" said Jinn-Aka as he clasped the forearms of the Emperor his crimson eyes glinting in the filtered light. As the Dominators stood to leave Vas-Sem swung back to face Jinn-Aka.

"Whatever awaits us at the outpost, I will bring to a swift conclusion. I have never failed in a mission." Vas-Sem's words were confident and sincere.

"Of that there is no doubt" answered Jinn-Aka a broad smile on his face. As the two warriors left the confines of the sanctuary Lord Senn cast a concerned glance at the Virtue.

"Will it be enough?" he asked.

"The plan is sound my Lord, it will not fail" answered the Virtue.

*

In the short time she had spent in the driftwood town Muyda could still not get used to sleeping in a bed, if it could be called a bed, with three other people. It was early morning and her breath formed a mist in the cold air. She rose quietly trying not to disturb the others and wrapped a blanket around her shoulders as she made her way to the hearth. She proceeded to add fresh timber to the fire. The crackling of the burning wood awoke Set.

"I'm sorry" apologised Muyda. "I didn't mean to wake you."

"That's OK" yawned Set as he stretched his arms. Muyda looked at him as he got dressed, his painfully thin body and thinning hair made him appear much older than his relatively young age. She remembered his kind eyes and soft voice that had saved her from herself when she had first arrived on Imercia.

After the initial visual shock of Imercia, Muyda's situation had overwhelmed her. In the pouring rain she had trudged through the mud down to the ocean's edge. She had knelt in the sand with the cold waves lapping around her legs. She no longer shivered with cold or felt the icy rain on her face, her body and mind numb to everything that surrounded her. She felt self pity that a woman who had had everything now knelt here before the world with nothing. She had lost her lover, her family, her home and her name. Her self-pity made her feel guilty. She had looked at the ocean somehow expecting it to give her answer to her predicament. She knew the only answer would lie in its depths. She was woken from her desperate state as a bony hand gently touched her shoulder. She remembered turning with a start only to relax on seeing the pale unthreatening frame of Set.

"You still have your soul. That is something they can never take from you." She recalled the words exactly. They had felt like a warm embrace pulling her back from the precipice. Set had led her back to his shack and had given her dry clothes and food and introduced her to the two elderly women who also lived there. They had showed such kindness to a complete stranger she had felt truly humbled. As she looked at the broken man before her now a tear crept down her cheek at the injustice of his life.

Muyda soon learnt the harsh world of the Murai. She joined the work detail the very next morning. The whole island of Imercia was covered in food crops apart from the small fortress where she had arrived and the mountainous outcrop at the far end of the island. It was the life of a Murai to work in the fields from dawn until dusk. Each Murai had to check in first thing in the morning and then again at the end of the rotation. Provided the crops were delivered on time and there had been no problems during the rotation, they were given a meagre food allowance. After cooking and eating their evening meal they retired totally exhausted. This cycle was the repeated rotation after rotation until they eventually gave in to hunger, sickness or exhaustion.

In this world of pain and misery Muyda had unexpectedly felt a reborn sense of purpose and friendship. For the first time in her life she had genuine friends that liked her for who she was, not what she could provide or do for them. She felt an overwhelming urge to protect them, to improve their lives, perhaps one rotation to deliver salvation. It had been these thoughts that had caused her to run to the aid of a young girl that had unfortunately spilled her basket under the watchful eye of a Reaver. He had lashed his metal studded whip across the girl's legs bringing her to the floor. As he raised his arm to strike her again, Muyda had thrown herself over the girl to protect her. The Reaver had paused for a brief moment and then unleashed a flurry of savage lashes across Muyda's back. Suitably impressed with his handiwork the Reaver strolled away leaving a blood soaked Muyda for dead behind him. All present had watched in horror as Muyda had taken the beating without as much as a whimper. Over the next few rotations the people of the Driftwood town had shared their food rations and many a stranger had visited each helping bathe and dress her wounds.

As she stood up in the small confines of the shack the tightness and soreness of the deeper wounds pulled at her skin and she winced at the pain.

"It's too early for you to be up and about" Set quietly whispered noticing Muyda's discomfort.

"Nonsense" replied Muyda. "This rotation is the meeting. It is more important than ever that I appear strong."

"It could be postponed Muyda" complained Set. "You have already done enough for the people here. You have given us all hope; they would understand if you were not yet ready." He added gently. Muyda sighed.

"I know they would my dear Set. I cannot wait. What I have to say must be said and said now." Set smiled. Despite her significant injuries Muyda was still a determined woman. Before the incident in the fields Muyda enquired after the leaders of the Murai. Although many in numbers the Murai had no official leader or community structure, life expectancy was short, just staying alive was difficult enough. There wasn't time for anything else to exist. The Murai were predominately a matriarchal society and did meet as a people from time to time where decisions were made by democratic vote.

These instances were few. It was just such a meeting Muyda had instigated.

*

"Is it broken?" enquired a deeply concerned Bok-Te.

"Pass me that wrench" said Vor-I. The replicator stretched out his hand towards his companion without removing his head from the engine bay. Bok-Te slapped the wrench into the outstretched hand which retracted it into the small space. Bok-Te had known Vor-I for some time. Good replicators were rare, so he had struck up a friendship in order to keep his sea blade running. Over time he had grown to like the little man and now he actually preferred his company to that of his Reavers. He admired the dedication he showed to his art despite his strange antics and antiquated beliefs.

He had explained to Bok-Te on more than one occasion about the era of great technology, when every person no matter what their status had a machine they could travel in. Vast machines flew in the sky and every household had machines that made tasks easier and more efficient. He had listened with interest but knowing clearly that his friend had lost his mind. The machines that the Dumonii still used were ancient that was definitely true. Vor-I claimed they were the last remaining examples of the previous technological marvels. The Dumonii in their supreme arrogance had long since lost the knowledge that created the machines. Now a handful of individuals like Vor-l, known as replicators, kept the remaining vehicles and machines operational by robbing parts from derelict husks. The fleet of sea blades had once numbered in the thousands. The harbour of Imercia now sheltered forty-three operational craft with various other disassembled bodies lying rusting on the quayside. It was Bok-Te's sea blade that the small replicator was now trying to keep from this metal graveyard.

Despite the clear skill and knowledge required to become an adept replicator, the position carried no official name in the Dumonii society and hence Vor carried the standard male suffix of 'l'. This also applied to the medicators who healed and enhanced the bodies of the Dumonii. Bok-Te thought this was extremely unfair. Only strength and prowess as a warrior or leader meant anything in their society. He suspected that the higher orders and his father included did not understand what these skilled technicians could do and how important it was to society. Perhaps it was because their civilization seemed to no longer rely on machines.

Vor-l hauled himself from the engine bay and turned to smile at his friend. His white crooked teeth stood out against the oil and grease that coated his face.

"I think that's it" he said proudly "Go give it a turn." Bok-Te moved into the cabin and pumped the priming handle several times before tentatively turning

72

the start key. The engine grumbled and coughed and then spluttered into life with a deep throaty growl. He beamed at his friend who was doing a strange dance with the wrench and punching the air.

"Brilliant!" yelled Bok-Te over the engine noise. "You truly are a mechanical genius" applauded the big Missionrai. He had been seriously concerned that his beloved sea-blade would have to be scrapped. He turned the start key again and the engine quietened.

"So" said an animated and elated Vor-l. "Now that I have worked my magic and breathed new life into this old heap, are you going to keep your promise and take me out fishing?" Bok-Te slapped the small man on the shoulder knocking him forward.

"Of course I am Vor. Go and get changed and I'll prep the old heap as you call it for a hunt." Without hesitating the small man leapt the side rail and ran up the quayside to the tower building to change. Bok-Te climbed the rail and walked along the small wing to the jetty where a jumble of nets lay piled. He looked back longingly at the old machine eager to take it out on the ocean once more.

Apart from small rowing boats and wooden kayaks the sea blades were the only transport capable of sea travel. The sea blade consisted of a central hull rounded at the prow where the cabin sat. Behind the cabin was a long rear deck with rails on either side. Extending from either side were stubby wings. Each wing housed a large rotor. On top of the cabin, accessed by a small ladder was the top deck also edged by rails. On the underside of the hull, and not visible when docked was a long keel. The keel ended in a long weighted lozenge. It was the large keel that gave the machine its name. When the wing rotors turned they created a cushion of air that raised the machine out of the water. It then revealed the blade-like keel which was the only piece of the craft that made contact with the sea when in flight. In the back of the keel was a hydro jet which gave it forward motion. The sea blade was incredibly fast and manoeuvrable. The ride was smooth as it glided on the air pocket, kept stable by the weighted blade even in rough weather. If only it was mechanically reliable.

Bok-Te untangled the net and laid it across the floating jetty. The net had lead weights along two sides and stank of the seaweed that still clung to it. He carefully folded it into a triangle and then repeated the process with the other two nets. He clambered back on board and up the ladder to the top deck. He opened the chamber on the swivel mounted net launcher and carefully inserted the net. He then vaulted down to the rear deck and walked to examine the rear mounted nail gun. It was a larger model of the hand held version carried by most warriors. It was just as unreliable but very effective when it did work. Bok-Te removed the large cylindrical magazine and unscrewed one side. The magazine was full of finger length metal spikes. He replaced the lid and slid the cylinder home. He flicked a switch on top of the gun and the in-built compressor hissed into action. Satisfied the weapons were functioning he jumped back to the jetty ready to untie the craft from its mooring.

As he bent down to untie the rope an over enthusiastic Vor-I came bounding down the quayside, a devilish grin etched onto his face.

"Do I get to drive?" asked Vor-I. He had changed out of his oil stained replicator garb into a tight fitting waterproof one piece which revealed his slightly portly figure. He hadn't however managed to remove the oil from his face.

"Why not" smiled Bok-Te "I'll need a good driver while I man the nets." Bok-Te untied the rope and both men climbed aboard the sea blade.

"Which direction are we heading?" asked Vor-I as he fired up the engine.

"Set a course for the Uxmal region" replied Bok-Te.

"What!" exclaimed Vor-I his eager excitement draining in a second "Not all the way to Uxmal, that's Kekken territory."

"Well what did you think we were going to hunt?" teased Bok-Te.

"I thought we would be after Sakurai or maybe even a Baraq, but not Kekken. Is it safe? I have heard stories about them, they hunt in packs and are….” He paused.

"Are what?" interrupted Bok-Te "Intelligent?"

"Yea" said Vor-l "That's what people say."

"Do you suppose these people have seen a Kekken? Do you think they have hunted them?"

"Have you?" blurted Vor-l.

"Of course I have" said Bok-Te offended by his friend's disbelief.

"Only you have never mentioned it before" continued Vor-l.

"Would you have believed me?" retorted Bok-Te. "I was near the Uxmal region the last time I was out. I saw a lone Kekken break the surface. I managed to catch up with it and get in front. I sent a cascade of nails into the creature but the body sank before I could get to it. Otherwise I would have brought it back and there would be no need for you and I to be out hunting now." Bok-Te's voice rose in volume.

"Okay, Okay," said Vor-l with renewed vigour. "Let's net ourselves a Kekken!" Bok-Te smiled as his friend guided the sea-blade out of the harbour. He didn't like lying to Vor-l, but it wasn't a complete lie. He had seen a Kekken, or at least it looked a lot like one. He couldn't possibly have chased it down on his own, that's why he needed Vor-l. He thought of the comments and praise he would receive when he returned with the corpse of a legendary Kekken, especially from his father the Emperor. His adrenaline pulsed as the replicator opened the throttle and the sea blade rose up like a metal beast and scythed through the ocean.

*

As Vas-Sem approached the assembled seated Reavers they stood and bowed. Ty-Sem remained seated on a supply crate meticulously cleaning his nail gun. This particular squad of Reavers was well known and respected on Son-Gebshu. Their leader, Vas-Sem's brother, was well liked by his men and together they proved a very effective unit. The men were all seasoned professionals and all eager to be on their way. Vas-Sem approached the seated Dominator towering over him. Ty-Sem ignored the big man.

"I am heading to the surface to fetch my brother" started Vas-Sem. Still the other man ignored him. "Take the squad and supplies to Morlok-Tun and wait for us there, I will not be long." At last Ty-Sem slowly looked up.

"Do not think to give me orders boy. You and I are equals despite your elevated birth" snapped Ty-Sem.

"They are not my orders you fool. They are the orders of the Emperor" countered the big man. Ty-Sem rose, his point made. He barked orders at the on-looking soldiers and they hurriedly started lifting the supplies towards the gate.

"How long will you be?" asked Ty-Sem.

"A rotation at most" sighed Vas-Sem. "But do not think of leaving Morlok-Tun without me" he added.

"I wouldn't dream of it" countered Ty-Sem as he joined the squad heading towards the gate. One by one they disappeared through the miasma. The humming noise emanating from the servillisors irritated the big Dominator and he hurried to enter the gate albeit from another direction.

Vas-Sem hurried through the fortress keen to retrieve his brother and be on his way. He knew Ty-Sem wouldn't leave without him but he didn't want to present him with the opportunity. He climbed steep stone steps and came out onto a long curtain wall which stretched out towards the harbour complex. The wall was the only link between the fortress and harbour defences that saved the Dumonii having to walk through the squalor of the driftwood town. He descended into the harbour buildings and entered the harbour master's office. The warrior was sitting with his legs outstretched on his desk. He nearly fell off his chair in his hurry to stand, shocked by the presence of a Dominator especially one as big as Vas-Sem.

"I am looking for Bok-Te" stated Vas-Sem simply.

"Um, I am not sure where he is; I have only just come on duty" he stuttered. "I think he has taken a blade out."

"Is there no log?" demanded Vas-Sem losing his patience. The nervous guard quickly thumbed through a large book on the table.

"Yes" he said relieved. "It says that he took a sea-blade out on a test run." He looked up at the big man knowing what the next question would be.

"Where did he go? And what time will he be back?" insisted Vas-Sem.

"It doesn't say" stammered the man "I can check the locator beacon" he suggested.

"Do it!" commanded Vas-Sem. The man hurried across the room to a huge machine with an array of switches, leads, plugs and a large glass screen. He plugged and unplugged a selection of connecting wires and flicked several switches. A feint red light began to pulse on the glass screen.

"It looks like he is heading towards the Uxmal region" said the anxious warrior. "You could always ask Dei-Su; he may know more than me as it was his shift before mine."

"Someone who knows more than you. I find that hard to believe." The sarcasm was lost on the nervous guard. "Where can I find Dei-Su?"

"He will be in the Murai town somewhere" offered the man cowering as if expecting a thump. Vas-Sem strode out of the office and the harbour master collapsed with relief. The Dominator exited the harbour complex through an unguarded side door into the chaos of the driftwood town. He walked carefully through the mud trying to find the optimal path through the sludge. As he rounded a cluster of small dwellings he stopped frozen to the spot as if paralysed. Muyda stood facing him. As surprised as she was to see her eldest son, it did not show and she greeted him courteously.

"Hello my son."

"I am not your son" replied Vas-Sem still in shock "My mother died when she threw away her name." He spat the words out with venom.

"Whatever has come to pass, the fact remains I gave birth to you Vas, so like it or not I am your mother" she said, her hackles rising.

"What do you want woman? I am in a hurry" he barked. Muyda sighed and relaxed, she knew her sons were lost to her long ago, but deep down there was always a glimmer of hope.

"I do not want to fight with you. I did not expect to see you here and I was taken by surprise that is all. I am sorry if I offended you." Muyda's tone was calm and measured. Vas-Sem relaxed slightly. "There was something I wanted to tell you before I left but never got the chance. Something you must know. Your father believes he is the Emperor of the prophecy." Vas-Sem stared in disbelief at his mother "He believes that one of my sons will return to overthrow him and bring about the end of the Dumonii."

"That's insane" protested Vas-Sem.

"You and I both know that" explained Muyda "He is becoming more unpredictable as he grows older; his mind is starting to play tricks on him. He will become suspicious of you and Bok."

"Lies" shouted Vas-Sem. "I will not listen to your lies. You are bitter that he cast you aside that is all. My father is a great man and I will serve him as best I can."

"I pray that your best is good enough my son" said Muyda moving towards the big man. He stepped back looking in disgust at his mother. He took one last look and walked off towards the fortress. "Whatever you have become my son, I will always love you." Muyda's words stung the Dominator and he shook his head trying to shake the encounter from his mind. He looked ahead and spotted a rotund Reaver ahead and focused his aggression.

"Dei-Su" shouted Vas-Sem.

"Yes, yes" choked the Reaver unsure why a huge Dominator had suddenly appeared from nowhere and was threatening him.

"Bok-Te, where did he go and when will he be back" demanded the Dominator.

"I don't know" apologised Dei-Su. "He often goes out on his own. He never records where or when he will be back" defended the man trying to hold himself together.

"Why not? Why don't you make him?" asked a puzzled Vas-Sem. The Reaver lent in close and whispered.

"He is the son of the Lord Emperor." Vas-Sem just stared at the man in disbelief.

"When he returns, have him travel to the Sagen-Ita gate immediately. It is of the utmost urgency" ordered Vas-Sem and he lent in close towards the shocked guard. "Tell him, Vas-Sem eldest son of the Lord Emperor requests his presence" he whispered. Dei-Su stumbled backwards and landed unceremoniously in the mud. The surrounding Murai were careful not to meet his scowl.

Although Muyda had known the feelings of her sons, to be confronted by it still hurt. She would never wish harm upon them, but it wouldn't hurt if there was unrest and distrust in the family.

Regaining her composure she entered the small hut where Set was waiting for her. They entered and the door was closed behind them. The matting on the floor was moved to reveal a makeshift ladder descending into the ground. Set climbed down and helped Muyda follow. They crawled through the cramped tunnel guided by the flickering light ahead. As they reached the end Set helped Muyda out into a large but low cavern. It was mostly natural apart from several alcoves that were clearly man made. The underground scene was dimly lit by multiple candles and Muyda could smell the sea in the damp air. About one hundred people were squashed into the cave. All stood quietly. One elderly woman stepped forward and clasped Muyda's hands in her own.

"Welcome" she said in a gentle but tired voice. "I am Danus-Mayrig and for this occasion I am the voice of those gathered."

"Thank You" said Muyda to the woman. "Thank you to all of you for coming to listen to what I have to say. I am Danus-Muyda, but some of you will know me by my previous name, Apos Senn." There were gasps amongst the listeners. "It is true that I once lived a life of comfort in a privileged position married to the Emperor, but that was another life. I have only been here a short while and I have been shown such kindness from people who have so little to give. My life and my future are here among the people of Imercia. I have not come here to preach to you. There have been too many words. I have come here to start a wave, a tidal wave of revolt." The gathered Murai looked at each puzzled. "This place, our home, Imercia, The Garden of the Gods, whatever you call it, it is the key to this world. Not only does it hold our lives in balance but those of our captors. Without the food we provide they would quickly starve." Danus-Mayrig stepped forward.

"What are you suggesting - that we destroy the crops?"

"No" answered Muyda. "I am suggesting we simply refuse them access to the food."

"And how do we do that?" shouted one of the crowd.

"By destroying the gate" answered Muyda.

"That would be suicide" shouted another. Muyda took a deep breath.

"I would not deny that some wouldn't make it, but what is our alternative? This is not a life that we lead; this is just existence. We are slaves and will continue to be so until the rotation we travel to the depths. Surely it is worth the sacrifice to attempt to live our lives freely?" There was a long silence.

"What did you have in mind?" asked Mayrig.

*

The two men were enjoying the thrill of the ride. The sea blade bounced along hugging the surface of the ocean like a skimming stone. Both men had childish grins etched across their faces.

"I'm going up top" shouted Bok-Te. Vor-I who had his hands firmly clamped on the steering wheel nodded his approval. Bok-Te reached into a cabinet and pulled out a harness made from webbing. He began to step into it and fasten buckles around his legs and waist. As he slung the straps over his shoulders the large pack that was attached slid into place on his back. Despite its bulk it was light to wear. "Give me a few moments to get settled and then slow her to a crawl" said Bok-Te leaning to speak in Vor-I's ear.

"Okay, will do" agreed the replicator. Bok-Te climbed the ladder to the top deck and picked up a hook attached to a cylindrical winch. He hooked the wire rope onto his harness and set a lever on the side of the machine to 'spool'. Checking he was firmly attached he pulled down hard on a rip cord hanging down from the backpack. The pack sprang into action as thin arms unfolded in all directions. As the arms snapped into position the material between them pulled tight and the wind caught the surface and lifted Bok-Te into the air. The giant kite slowly lifted him further as the geared winch gradually spooled out the cable. Within moments Bok-Te was flying high above the sea blade below.

Vor-I slowed the craft to a crawl and stuck his head out of the cabin to look up at his friend. He gave the thumbs up signal which Bok-Te copied. With the sea blade locked on course in a slow creep, Vor-I climbed the ladder on to the top deck. There was nothing but ocean in every direction.

"How is it up there?" shouted Vor-I.

"Windy" replied Bok-Te. Despite the slow speed of the towing sea blade the huge area of the kite kept the big warrior aloft with ease, dangling in the wind at the end of the wire rope.

"Can you see anything?" asked Vor-I. Bok-Te scanned the surrounding ocean. It was fairly calm but he couldn't see any signs of life.

"Throw in the bait" he shouted down to his friend. Bok-Te watched the small man pick up the bucket and walk to the side. He swung the load backwards and then released it over the side. The bucket landed in the ocean with a splash.

"You're only supposed to throw the bait in, not the bucket as well" laughed Bok-Te. Vor-I looked up and smiled, shrugging his shoulders. The bait consisted of fish bits and blood and what hadn't sunk with the bucket was now floating on the surface. Bok-Te looked closely around, his black eye implants removing the glare, giving him a clear view of the ocean. Out to port he caught a glimpse of movement in his peripheral vision. He focused on the area. There was a dark shape moving towards the sea blade at speed, although at this height it looked no bigger than a man. A kekken thought Bok-Te. He hoped it was.

"Get me down" he shouted to Vor-I. "I think we may have something port side." Ignoring his friend's command to bring him down, Vor-I raced to the side rail and looked out over the ocean. He couldn't see anything. Up above Bok-Te could clearly see the shape moving ever closer on a direct line to the sea blade.

"It's getting closer" he yelled. "Get me down start the winch."

"Okay, Okay" grumbled Vor-I. He turned and booted a lever on the winch with his foot. The gears bit and complained at the strain and then slowly began to reel in the flying Bok-Te. As Vor-I turned, a creature leapt from the ocean landing on the top deck, stunning both men. Before either could understand what was happening the creature had sunk its needle like teeth into Vor-I's shoulder and sliced its talons across his stomach.

"No" screamed Bok-Te as his friend stumbled back across the deck clutching his belly, still in shock, his fingers desperately trying to keep his intestines within the confines of his body. He slumped back on the floor, blood pouring from both wounds. The creature walked towards him. Bok-Te drew his side arm and switched on the compressor. It whistled as it activated and the creature looked up at the airborne prey.

The creature was about the same height as a man. It had a rounded head with two glassy teardrop shaped eyes on either side, two vertical slits where a nose should be and a hideous mouth that stretched all the way around its face. The grim maw was lined with razor sharp needle teeth. A series of fins ran from the top of its head down its back and along its powerful tail. It had arms and legs like a human also, although the legs seemed less formed. Its arms however were very powerful and ended in long webbed fingers with lethal black talons. Its dark grey skin glistened in the light. The kekken stared at Bok-Te and hissed. The creature sent a chill through the warrior.

His finger reacted first, squeezing the trigger of the nail gun. The compressor whined and whirred but nothing else happened. As Bok-Te removed the cartridge the kekken had reached his friend and with ease picked him up and threw him like a rag doll to the lower deck. Vor-I screamed as he landed on his bitten shoulder, his intestines now spilling onto the wooden floor. Bok-Te cursed and slammed the cartridge against his leg and shoved it back into the gun. He aimed and squeezed the trigger. This time the gun pulsed into life sending a shower of metal spikes towards the kekken. It leapt to one side but was not quick enough to avoid all of the deadly shards. Several nails pierced deep into its soft skin. The creature let out a shriek of high pitched clicks as it fell to the floor.

Bok-Te was still being reeled in towards the blood stained deck as he noticed more dark shapes approaching the sea-blade. He looked at his friend who was sobbing with pain. He had to get to him quickly, but no sooner had the thought occurred to him another beast leapt from the ocean onto the deck. It gave a glance skyward to the giant kite and then dived towards the stricken man. Bok-Te fired again, metal spikes tracing the creature around the deck as it sought to avoid them. It dived into the cabin for cover. As it did another much larger kekken leapt onto the rear deck swooshing sea water over the stricken man. Vor-I screamed as the thing loomed over him. He reached out a hand and pleaded for his life. The creature lunged forward and sank its teeth into his arm. With violent force it jerked its head to one side ripping Vor-I's arm apart. The poor replicator shouted in agony. Bok-Te carefully aimed his weapon and fired a volley of shards. The metal spikes thunked into the chest of his friend and his pain filled eyes glazed over.

Bok-Te gritted his teeth and opened up the nail gun in fury at the big creature. It too dived for cover but not before several spikes embedded themselves in its tail. The gun clicked repeatedly indicating it was out of ammunition. He hurled the gun in protest into the cabin where the two creatures skulked. He had to free himself from the tether and the kite before he was dragged helplessly into the fray. The two kekken emerged from the cabin making guttural clicking noises to each other. As he came over the rear deck, still the height of four men above it, he drew his short curved sword and clamped it in his teeth. He yanked the release cord on the kite which tumbled away into the wind. At the same time his other hand pulled the clip releasing him from the tether. He plummeted towards the deck, and as he did the smaller kekken leapt to meet him mouth wide and claws outstretched.

The trained Missionrai was a different target compared to the unarmed and unprepared Vor-l. Bok-Te twisted the blade in his hands and landed with a thud on the charging creature. His weight crushing it beneath him and cushioning his landing, allowing him to roll to one side leaving his sword buried deep in the body of the kekken and firmly lodged in the wooden deck. He moved back and brought himself up into a crouched position staring at the big kekken ahead of him.

The creature looked at the man; thin filmy eyelids closed and opened renewing the moisture of its orbs. It opened its savage mouth slightly, saliva dripping from its teeth. It made a series of clicks like it was attempting to speak with its crouching prey.

It leapt from the cabin with blistering speed. Bok-Te rocked backwards onto his back and shot out both legs catching the charging animal in the midriff. With a swift push and the creature's own momentum he launched it over his head and into the ocean. Bok-Te scrambled to his feet and looked at the mounted nail gun. It would be too close he thought. He ran for the ladder and in two steps was on the top deck. The kekken was already out of the water. Bok-Te grabbed the handle of the net launcher and swang it to bear on the creature. He pulled the release lever and the net enveloped the attacking kekken. The net tangled around its limbs as it thrashed furiously to free itself. Bok-Te leapt to the lower deck and as he landed sent a fierce kick towards the captured creature. He bent down and heaved his sword from the dead kekken. He stood over the foul creature which had now stopped struggling. He put his boot across its neck and flipped the sword over in the air catching it by the blade. He swung it down striking the creature square on the head with the pommel.

He fastened the net securely around the unconscious creature and hauled it to the rear of the deck. He tied a rope to the railings and hefted the body overboard. It hung in the net half submerged behind the sea-blade. Bok-Te looked out at the ocean squinting slightly. It was another black shape. He jumped behind the mounted nail gun and activated the compressor.

Chapter 4 - The Black River

Var turned onto his back still kicking his fins. There was nothing behind him. He felt like he was being followed but he couldn't see any signs. His mind raced. He thought of his father and his brothers, his friend Astur and of all the unknowing widows awaiting him back at the pods. The image of the baited trap entered his thoughts and he saw Astur's father floating with his throat slit. It had to be Rickron. He was the only unknown in this situation. Whoever or whatever had caused this bloodshed would pay. Var promised this to himself.

As he neared the pods he started to recognize his surroundings. He also noticed somebody swimming out towards him. As he neared he recognized his father. They met and embraced. Var was overwhelmed with emotion, relieved to see him still alive. He held his father tightly not wanting to let go. He forced himself to pull away and signed to his father.

    <<BROTHERS>>

    <<SAFE>> signalled Gednu. Both exhausted the two men swam back towards the village.

As Var appeared in the pool his two brothers eagerly grabbed him and pulled him into the pod. They clung to him desperately. His mother stood by, a tear rolling down her cheek.

"Thank the gods" she sobbed. Var's father followed him out of the pool and gave him a manly slap on the shoulder.

"Did anyone else make it back?" asked Var.

"Astur made it" said his father. "He came back not long before you. He didn't stop, he went straight home. I think it's going to be a while before what has happened sinks in for all of us. No one else made it back" he said sadly.

"I need to speak with him" suggested Var.

"Give him some time son" said his father. Var sighed deeply.

"I still can't believe this has happened. That bastard Rickron will pay with his life for this" growled Var clenching his fists.

"You must be careful son. It is natural to want to find someone to blame, but we cannot cast accusations until we know for sure what happened. Anyone could have set that bait field, it may have simply been bad timing." Gednu could see the anger rising in his son's face.

"Maybe" started Var "But how do you explain all of the dead tribesmen floating with their throats cut. Astur's father was one of them" he exclaimed. His father looked hard at Var and then cast a concerned glance to his wife.

"That I didn't know" he confessed. "We must travel to Beng Melea and seek the guidance of their elders."

"I'll get my things" said Var moving towards his chamber.

"We will go" said Gednu, "but not now. It will be dark soon. Tomorrow we must tell the women of the tribe that their loved ones will not be coming back. They must have time to mourn. We will go on the morrow, now get some rest my son." With reluctance Var agreed and made his way to his room, kissing his mother on the cheek as he passed. He laid on his bed knowing sleep would elude him. He didn't want to sleep - he wanted to act.

*

Astur climbed out from the pool and walked to the living area. His mother and sister were busy sewing.

"You're back early" said his mother not looking up from her work. Bronsur looked up at her brother and saw the tears streaming down his face. She put her hand on her mother's who then looked up noticing the look of concern on her daughter's face. She turned quickly and immediately saw the distress in her son. She jumped up and hugged him. Astur sobbed into her shoulder. Bronsur didn't know how to react. She had never seen her brother like this. He was normally so strong and assured. After what seemed like ages Astur sat, his head hung low. He wiped away the tears, now embarrassed by his emotional state.

"Tell us what happened my dear" said his mother softly.

"They are all dead" he said simply. Now it was the turn of Bronsur and his mother to be in shock.

"Who's dead? Where is your father?" said Almay, the concern clearly showing in her voice.

"We were attacked" said Astur quietly. "It was a murmur..." he started to continue.

"Where is everyone? Did it get them all? What about your father?" demanded Almay. Astur tried to ignore the barrage of questions.

"He is safe, although we got separated. I am not sure if anyone else made it back."

"Great Gods!" exclaimed his mother holding tightly onto Bronsur's hand. Astur stood and walked towards the pool. "Where are you going? You need to tell us what happened" screamed his mother, tears flooding down her face. Bronsur put her arm around her mother and they heard the splash as Astur disappeared into the sea.

"He'll tell us soon enough mother. I think he needs some time to understand what happened himself."

*

Var didn't sleep, the horrific events of the hunt spinning over in his mind. He had risen early and pleaded with his father to accompany him as he visited the widows of the village to inform them of the news. His father had refused. It was getting late once again and Var was desperate to get out and do something. What, he didn't know, but anything would be better than just waiting for his father's return. He donned his skin and stared at the bio-lung he had taken from the body of Vieto, Astur's father. He was reluctant to wear the dead man's rig again, but the urge for action was too great and he fitted the lung to his back, bit on the mouthpiece and dived into the pool.

He swam the short distance to a nearby pod and quietly popped his head up into the pool. He climbed out and walked through the doorway. Bronsur was at the stove preparing a meal.

"Hi" whispered Var. Bronsur turned with a start, clutching at her heart.

"Var! You scared me." With the surprise fading she stood and hugged him awkwardly. She had liked him for some time but he had never seemed interested. She was terrified of doing or saying the wrong thing. The only thing she could think of now was how relieved she was to see him still alive. "I had thought the worst. Astur had said that everyone had died. I wanted to visit but I wasn't sure I should."

"Tell me about it" declared Var. "My father has not allowed me out. I have been going crazy cooped up in my pod. He said to give you and your family some time, but I couldn't wait either." Her heart soared. "Is Astur home?" The simple question ended her romantic thoughts.

"He left late last night. We have not seen him since. He was very upset. I've never seen him like this before" she said sadly.

"Yes" said Var. "It has been difficult to keep a level head."

"I'm sorry Var; where are my manners? Are your brothers and your father..." her words trailed off. Var saw her struggle.

"They made it back safely Bron" he smiled. "Look, if you're not busy perhaps you and I can go to the nest. It would be good to talk to someone, if you don't mind?" Bronsur tried not to smile. That would have been inappropriate. Despite the circumstances she felt hopeful.

"No of course not" she replied quickly. "I'll just take this food to mother and then we'll go."

*

Astur sat with his back against a large rock on the edge of the village. He was staring at the pile of beacons that lay at his feet. 'There was nothing I could have done' he told himself. It didn't matter how many times he repeated it, he could not escape the guilt of his inaction. He cast a glance over his shoulder back towards the pods. He had neglected his duties. As an Outrider he should be there organizing things, going to check for survivors. He couldn't stand to look at anyone. Even his mother and sister had reminded him of the shame he bore. He must make amends. It was the only thought that had any clarity. He would have to lay the beacons otherwise Rickron would kill his father and the others. There would be no harm in that, there was nothing of value in the village, and it was certainly no longer a threat. As soon as his father was safe he would turn and kill the murderous Rickron, even if that meant his own demise. That surely would atone for his lack of action so far.

He picked up the bundle of beacons and headed away from the village. On the outskirts he planted the first beacon stick. He swam on unwinding the cord and planting the next. It was some time before the great rift came into sight. Even at a spool's length away he could feel the current against him and see the plant life sway in the direction of the awesome Black River. Astur tied off the last of the beacons and scanned the area for a good vantage point. There was relatively little cover; the closer to the rift the less of anything. It was as if the Black River sucked the life from around it. To the East there was a small outcrop of boulders. That would have to do.

As Astur swam towards the rocks he was suddenly aware of a shadow overhead. He looked up blinking several times not convinced of what he was seeing. Way above him and travelling in an arc was a large circular cage. Attached to the leading edge was a massive hook and trailing out behind was a huge chain which snaked its way into the distance across the Black River.

He stared in complete disbelief as the huge metal ball came closer. He could now make out several figures inside the cage. The mass of metal continued to descend and eventually the large iron hook thudded into the seabed not far from where Astur was treading water. The large ball cage hammered down behind it. The chain despite its enormous weight and bulk was slowly being pulled by the current of the great rift. The force of the water slowly dragged the contraption back towards the edge of the canyon, scarring the ocean floor as it went. The men inside the cage swam out of the opening at the top of the cage and all piled on to the giant hook. They were lending their own weight in the hope that the hook would bite. Sure enough the rusty shell encrusted hook sank into the sand and secured itself in the bedrock.

Up above Astur saw a dozen more metal globes descend. He watched completely awestruck as one by one they pounded into the seascape. One cage nearby was getting perilously close to the edge. The men were desperately jumping and kicking the hook. A group of men already landed were on their way to help the struggling tribesmen. The powerful current caught the ball and chain and dragged it over the edge. It disappeared swiftly into oblivion. The stranded men fought hard to get back from the drop clearly terrified and exhausted by the effort.

As the first landing party neared, Astur could see they were Eburus and his stomach knotted as he recognized the tall figure of Rickron. He mustered his courage and he swam out looking for his father amongst the other groups. There was no sign of him. Astur twisted the handle of his harpoon and the spear point shot out as he swam towards Rickron. This time he would act, this time he would not fail. As he approached Rickron held up his hand and the following warriors fanned out around the lone Enki outrider.

<<Beacons>> signed Rickron.

<<Father>> signed Astur thrusting his harpoon towards the Eburus leader.

<<Safe>> signalled Rickron completely un-phased by the sharp point at this throat. Astur clenched the harpoon tightly and looked into the eyes of his enemy. He knew then that everything was a lie. He was about to lunge when a warrior behind him swam in quickly and stabbed a small spine into Astur's neck. Astur tried to remove the spike but his hand only made it halfway. He felt his body spasm as the neurotoxin from the poison spine spread through his body. Astur floated completely paralysed. The Eburus warriors smiled and laughed behind their breathing apparatus as they filed past him, following the beacons back towards the Enki village. Astur tried to scream. In his silent prison of his mind he now realized what he had done.

Rickron removed the harpoon from Astur's frozen hand by unfolding each finger. He then rammed the harpoon into the seabed. Another warrior handed him a length of rope and he tied one end around the harpoon and the other around Astur's leg, anchoring him to the spot.

*

Bronsur could not believe what Var had told her. He was sat close with his arm around her trying to comfort her as the news of her father's death sunk in. He surveyed the interior of the nest wishing that it was a different situation that had brought him this close to Bronsur.

"I'm sorry" sobbed Bronsur. "I must look a mess."

"That's not possible" comforted Var. Bronsur managed a smile. It was true, even under the tears and red eyes Bronsur's beauty shone through.

"I know this isn't the right time" started Var clearly uncomfortable with what he was about to say. "I wanted to ask you something." Bronsur placed a hand on his cheek which relaxed him. Behind them came a noise from the large plunge pool and they both turned to see three Eburus warriors climb menacingly from the pool. Var leapt to his feet drawing his serrated knife and ushered Bronsur behind him as he recognized the black and white markings. The first man removed his mouthpiece.

"We only want the girl. Hand her over and you can be on your way." The man had thinning hair and two front teeth missing. He had a long harpoon in his hand and clearly no intention of letting anyone go. Var Laughed.

"I think not" he said assuredly. Var's confidence unsettled the three warriors. The other two, also with harpoons, spread out around the couple. Var edged backwards his leg touched against a long wooden seat. He carefully stepped over it and waited. The leading Eburus warrior approached and as he came within range Var flipped the bench towards him with his foot. The warrior turned his back to take the impact on his shoulder and the bench clattered harmlessly to the floor. The guard lifted his arm raising his harpoon into a throwing position. He launched the weapon. Without hesitation Var rolled forward under the weapon and leapt, pivoting on his left foot whilst spinning his other in a wide arc. His foot caught the warrior square in the jaw knocking him from his feet. The other Eburus warrior rushed in and threw his harpoon. Var side stepped but the razored barb glanced his arm cutting through his skin and the flesh beneath. The first man rose and wiped the blood from his mouth. In the melee Var had separated himself from Bronsur. The third man had her hold with a knife to her throat and was dragging her towards the pool.

"Get your hands off her!" yelled Var.

"Or what?" laughed the warrior. Bronsur looked longingly at Var.

"I will come for you Bron" said Var, desperately looking for a way past the two men blocking his path.

"Don't take too long" said Bronsur forcing a smile. The guard holding her shoved in her mouthpiece and bundled her into the water.

The two advancing men drew their knives. Var turned and sprinted for the harpoon that jutted out of the nest wall. The two men followed. He reached the weapon but could not draw it free as the barb held it firmly within the wall. He quickly reached up and grabbed a bone stay breaking it away from the framework. As he turned he rammed the jagged bone into the advancing man. The sharp splintered bone tore out through the man's back. The other warrior halted his charge as Var used the dying man as a shield. Var glanced down and he could see a blade jutting from his thigh. It had not gone deep but the pain was still intense. He let the dead body slump to the floor and grabbed the handle of the knife in his leg. He wrenched it free with a growl. He wasted no time and advanced on the Eburus warrior, his blood stained knife flashing up and down. The warrior tried to fend off the savage blows but Var's blades kept biting. The warrior stumbled backwards sprawling onto the floor, his weapon skittering from his hand, the myriad of wounds on his arms finally taking their toll. Var landed on the helpless man, his knife across his throat.

"This one's for Vieto" he said, as his blade sliced through the jugular. Var grabbed the dying mans tunic and sliced a strip of material away. He tied it tightly around his leg, sheathed his knife and dived into the pool.

Even in the fading light the chaos of the village was apparent. There were people everywhere, some struggling, others being led away. The Eburus were taking the entire population. Var scanned the area for Bronsur. He couldn't make her out in all the confusion.

He swam, hugging the seabed and using all available cover to make his way up the hill unnoticed. He neared his parents pod and decided to make a sprint for it. His powerful legs kicked and within moments he was heading up into the pool. He had to warn his family and then he would go after Bronsur.

As he emerged from the pool he felt a sharp object touch the back of his neck. He saw his two brothers stood in the doorway; both had knives in their hands, blood dripping from the blades.

"It's OK father, it's Var!" shouted Mido. The harpoon tip withdrew and Var climbed from the pool to see his father behind him smiling.

"Are you OK son?" asked a concerned Gednu seeing the blood on his tunic.

"I'm fine and you?"

"Nothing the boys and I couldn't handle" he said gesturing towards the dead tribesman on the floor.

"They've taken Bron father; they are taking all of the women from the village."

"Then we must act quickly" stated Gednu.

"Even with the best current behind us there is no way the four of us can take on the whole Eburus tribe." There was a pause as Gednu realized the truth of his son's words. "You must make it to Beng Melea and tell them what has happened. They are sure to help" said Var.

"That's if they have not already suffered the same fate" said his mother. The fear on all their faces was clear. Gednu broke the silence.

"We will go to the next village and rally the Outriders. Var, shadow the Eburus and see where they are taking the women. Do not engage them my son. I will return as soon as I can with help and we will put an end to this treachery. There is no way across the Black River so they will have to move through Enki territory somewhere." He clasped his son's arms. "Povian be with us all" he murmured.

Gednu led his two sons and his wife out into the madness of the night. The light had all but faded. The moonlight now danced over the shadows that crept through the village. The family swam quickly, keeping together and staying low in an attempt to make their way North. As Gednu led his family through the Velp fields a shadow rapidly approached from below.

Gednu noticed the Eburus warrior but too late. He tried to block the strike, but the hunting warrior had followed the family and had timed his attack to perfection. The long metal staff he was carrying slammed into the side of Gednu's head instantly knocking him out. The assailant swivelled his body to block the path of the remaining family. The rest would be easy he thought, two kids and a woman. He twisted the end of the staff and a sharp blade appeared reflecting in the half light. Before he could even think about his next move the two brothers had made theirs. They dashed around the surprised figure with energetic speed like small fish goading a bigger predator. As they swam their hands darted out and back with equal speed. Within moments the lifeless body of the warrior floated before them. A cloud of blood was slowly enveloping him, as it oozed from the dozen or more stab wounds in his body. Muadin swam towards the body her knife drawn. She sliced through both breather pipes and kicked out at the carcass. She swam to her husband who was starting to wake. As Gednu slowly came around he found himself staring into the eyes of his wife. He smiled.

<<MUST GO>> she indicated. The family closed in and quickly disappeared into the gloom.

*

Var made his way up the vast underwater mountain. He had been careful not to encounter the Eburus on his way, although every fibre of his being had ached for revenge. He watched from his vantage point as the tribesmen lead

106

the Enki women in a long procession out of the village. With his enhanced vision he could make out the line of beacons they had planted which stretched in the direction of the great rift. He swam keeping his distance staying level with the last of the line. As they moved closer to the Black River, Var became more anxious. A thousand questions assailed his mind. He felt the gentle nudge of current which told him they were getting close to the rift. He decided to move in closer. He swam quickly kicking his fins rapidly but with small movements so as not to draw attention. As he neared the line of people he could clearly see Bronsur, four in from the back. He looked ahead and then gasped as he saw the floating figure of his friend tethered to a harpoon. Anger rose inside him and he tried to quell it, knowing it would cloud his judgement. He waited for the last man to pass his hapless friend and then swam towards him.

Astur stared unblinking at his friend, his body still paralysed. Inside the shell of his body his mind was in torment. He had wanted his heart to stop beating to end his misery. He had seen the women of his tribe pass him as prisoners, followed by his mother and his sister. Led to the cages by the very beacons he had planted. Now he looked in utter desolation at his friend as he shook his body and frantically signed to him. The pain in his mind blurred his vision.

Var drew his knife and severed the tether holding Astur. He then pulled the harpoon from the seabed. Despite the mental barriers he had put in place, the sight of his friend staked to the floor had caused his anger to boil over. He raged inside and his grip tightened around the harpoon.

He stared out at the bizarre scene that unfolded before him. The tribesmen and the captured women were clambering into the metal cages. A warrior on the nearest cage was stood above the hook. He had a handle in each hand and was frantically winding. The hand winch was slowly retracting the giant hook from the sea floor. As it slowly lost its purchase the cage swung violently to the left. Rock and dust clouded the water where the hook had erupted and the tip of the hook now gauged a deep line in the cliff top as the force of the Black River pulled the assembly over the edge. The cage fell sharply and then quickly withdrew into the darkness. All along the line the warriors were waiting their turn to free the hook that held them to the cliff top. Two more cages swung out and disappeared into the murky depths. Var could see the look of terror on the faces of those inside as they vanished.

Var kicked hard and headed towards the next cage where Bronsur was struggling inside. A warrior straddled the hook and was winding it in slowly. He looked up to see Var approaching. He doubled his effort spinning the handle as fast as he could. The hook reared slightly and the cage lurched back. The warrior looked up once more and as he did the razor sharp harpoon thudded into his chest.

A second warrior climbed out from the top of the cage as Var reached the metal hook. Var turned quickly just in time to see the metal cage next in line break its hold and swing towards them. He dived for the cage and gripped it firmly. The other metal ball slammed into it knocking it loose from its mooring. The force veered them out into the rift sending the emerging warrior tumbling away into the watery void. Var desperately clung to the cage, the current trying to rip him free from the spherical prison. An Eburus warrior inside the cage saw the unwanted passenger and raised his leg to stamp on Var's fingers. As he stamped Var released his grip with that hand. The brutal current immediately flipped him over smashing him into the cage. There was a hiss as the breathing containers ruptured. Var looked into the cage and saw Bronsur. Her hands and legs were bound. He looked up to see the guard attempt another stomp. As he tried Var reached into the cage grabbing the warrior's ankle. The current tugged at his body and the weight pulled the struggling man's leg out through the bars, his body halting his fall. Var now dangled perilously, his grip slipping on the protruding leg of the helpless guard. Var released his right hand and grabbed his knife and plunged it deep into the man's thigh. He revelled in the pain that flashed across his face. He held firmly onto the knife handle and released his other hand attempting to climb back towards the cage. The force of the current was too great as it pounded Var's body. The knife sliced through the soft flesh of the trapped leg throwing Var out into the rift.

He kicked his legs fiercely, clawing at the water with his arms in a hopeless attempt to reach the cage. But the prison and Bronsur had already vanished into the darkness. The current tumbled Var over and over as he fought to stabilize himself. He tried to control the panic that was rising inside. The speed of the current was phenomenal and within a few moments he had travelled many spools. He looked to either side but there was no sign of the rift walls, there was no sign of anything. Beneath him was a foreboding blackness waiting to drag him down into its depths.

Var focused his thoughts. His main bio-lung was cracked giving him little time to decide on his next move. He had his emergency breather but changing it in this river was too risky. He turned slightly to one side and started to kick out with his fins. His plan was to try and move with the flow slowly making his way to the Western edge of the rift. If he could make it there and if he could find some Velp he could make his way back up following the line of the chasm and intercept the Eburus.

Var's body ached. He had until now ignored the wounds on his leg and shoulder, but as his adrenaline evaporated, tiredness crept in to his limbs. He knew that if he stopped swimming it would be all over and he would be lost. He had swum for ages, the Black River carrying him a vast distance. All of his muscles were burning with effort. He longed to stop the pain but his mind and his desire for survival pushed him on. His injured shoulder was now all but useless, the blood draining his energy and life-force. He looked ahead and he could see light. Ahead of him was the never ending Western wall of the rift. Renewed hope helped him close on his goal. He powered forward with every last ounce of effort and eventually made it over the top of the underwater cliff. A few more kicks and he was free of the nightmare river.

He swam over the scoured seabed to a nearby rock. He replaced his broken breather with his emergency unit. He breathed heavily, his body racked with pain and desperate for rest. He knew his small breather wouldn't give him that long and he needed another solution. He surveyed his surroundings. Apart from a few scattered rocks there was nothing but sand. He started out again at a slow pace, his body complaining even at this much reduced tempo. He swam inward but tried to keep the great rift in view to his right.

Despite his weakened state he covered a great distance before the breather started to fail. He knew it was going as the unit no longer filled his lungs with the precious oxygen he needed. There was only one choice left. Surface. Everything he had ever heard and ever been taught by the Wordkeeper told him otherwise. The ocean peoples were not permitted to break the surface of the water. Those that had tried had never returned. What lay above the ocean waves was unknown. The fear of this was equal to the fear of drowning. 'No it is not my time' thought Var. 'Nothing could be worse than swallowing the salty brine into my lungs'. He took one last breath and kicked towards the surface.

The light became intense as he headed upwards. He could feel the temperature change and the pressure reduce as he rose. He looked up and saw a large dark shape above. He broke through the ocean surface gasping for air as he did. The warm and bright light shocked his senses. He looked across at what was obviously causing the dark shape. It was a vessel of some kind, unlike anything he had ever seen. On the back of the craft stood what looked like a man. He stood pointing some sort of device in his direction. The machine made a high pitched noise and several projectiles whooshed into the water around Var. One metal shard pierced his side. His senses still in chaos, his primal reactions took over and he gulped a breath and dived. As he swam down he saw a dozen more objects trace their way into the water leaving a trail of bubbles. He twisted and turned trying to avoid the spikes. They barely missed him except one that embedded itself in his fin. He swam under the vessel and slowly edged his nose out of the water. He breathed carefully trying not to make a sound. He swam gently around the craft trying to get a glimpse of the strange man. He looked up and saw the armoured man holding on to the rails of the vessel. Their eyes met briefly. The armoured man swung his arm and a hook landed dangerously close in the water. The man proceeded to haul in the weapon. Whoever he was he certainly wasn't friendly and had made his intentions quite clear. Var was past the point of exhaustion whatever action he was going to take would be now or never.

He brought his arms forward and dived once more. He looked up to the surface to the shimmering outline of the man. He kicked his fins and launched himself up through the water. He shot out of the water and grabbed the surprised man by his armour and hauled him overboard. Without delay he turned the flailing man over and kicked again. The two men descended rapidly into the depths. The armoured man tried desperately to land a punch on the tribesman. Var had kept himself at arm's length, avoiding the blows. He kept his grip and looked into the young man's eyes, his face straining to hold his breath. Despite his size and strength he was no match for Var in his own environment. The big man's lungs were bursting. He finally gave out a breath and the sea quietly took hold of him. The lifeless body of Bok-Te stared back at Var. In the last seconds Var had felt something for the man. He wasn't sure what, but he felt a degree of regret at having to kill him. His own lungs now desperate for air, he swam back to the surface.

He hauled himself onto the craft. He held his stomach as he tried to refrain from emptying the contents as he viewed the grisly scene on board. Var collapsed to his knees staring at the mutilated bodies. A low clicking noise made him turn around. On the back of the boat was a creature like those that lay dead. It was obviously a creature of the sea but not one he had seen before. He stood and hauled the netted animal onto the deck. He walked across and retrieved a short sword.

The animal made what seemed like a more agitated noise as he approached. Whatever it was the armoured man that had tried to kill him had obviously killed the others like it and netted this one. The other man who lay with his guts torn open, Var could not explain. There had been too much death today thought Var as he knelt beside the captured creature. He cut through the net with the sword. With several bonds cut the kekken clawed its way out and stood before him. The creature moved its lipless mouth revealing a gruesome set of teeth. Var stepped back not so sure he had made the right decision.

The creature threw its head back and let out a shrill wail followed by clicking noises in its throat. It then turned its bulbous eyes on Var. The creature moved its arm across its chest and made a symbol with its talons. Var gasped as he realized the abomination before him was trying to communicate in the sign language of the ocean tribes. The animal repeated the action.

<<Friend>>

Var stared wide eyed. He replied with the same sign.

<<Friend>>

The creature blinked and then with lightening speed it lashed out a claw at Var. The razor sharp nail cut into Var's forehead and down through his eyebrow and across his cheek. The speed and surprise caused Var to fall backwards onto the deck. He lay there staring up at the sky marvelling at its beauty, expecting the final blow.

There was nothing he could do about it. His body and mind had at last given in to the assault they had endured. Nothing happened. He heard a splash as the creature dived into the ocean. He stared in amazement at the soft clouds that drifted overhead and he gently drifted away with them.

Chapter 5 – The Magta

Var stirred and opened his eyes. He moved slightly and felt the pull of his wounds. He was lying on a large bed covered by a warm fur pelt. The bed was at one side of the circular room. The single roomed building was constructed of stone to about head height with wooden rafters supporting a conical roof. In the centre of the dwelling was a fire pit surrounded by large stones. There were various furs and clothes hung around the walls and a large table with assorted pots and pans. Var could also make out a door partly hidden behind a hung pelt. He sat up surveying the room and grabbed at his side as the pain flared. The wound was neatly bandaged as was the stab wound on his leg. The cut on his shoulder had a strange smelling poultice rubbed into it. He rubbed his eyes blinking at the object he had just noticed. How could he have missed it? Leant against the end of the bed was an enormous axe. The weapon had butterfly blades which were made from a golden metal. They were engraved, although time had started to fade the lines. The wooden haft was wrapped with a rope handle and capped at either end with golden metal spikes. What made it stand out was its sheer size. It was almost as tall as Var. He stood and moved towards it. His hand was barely large enough to wrap around the grip, as he tried to lift it the door squeaked and a hand moved the pelt to one side.

"That's too big for you little man" said the person stooping to enter the hut. Var sat back on the bed in astonishment. The man that had entered would have no trouble in picking up the axe. Against his massive bulk it looked insignificant. The giant entered the hut and stood to his full height. He was at least a full torso taller than Var. He stood with both hands on his hips smiling at the bewildered Var. His arms were the size of a normal man's thighs. He wore metal vambraces over a fur cuff, with an animal skin jerkin covered by a battered cuirass. It had obviously seen a lot of action. He had intricate tattoos on his upper arms. They were not the crude coloured camouflage markings like that of the ocean peoples but beautifully coloured and complicated designs. On his legs he wore fur trousers with leather strapping around the calves. His face was weathered, although his bright blue eyes hinted at the vigorous life force that stirred behind them. He had grey hair covering his top lip and chin. Several lengths hung down under his chin, tied and beaded. The only other thing apart from his colossal size that set him apart from a normal man was his scalp. He had no hair but instead what looked like bony lumps which got smaller towards the back of his head. A couple at the front resembled small horns although all were covered in skin.

Var was aware he had been staring mouth open for some time. He stood and offered his hand towards the giant man.

"I am Var Son-Gednu Bay-Enki." The giant grasped Var's hand totally enveloping it.

"That's a bit of a mouthful" he laughed, "I am Gero." Var smiled.

"You can call me Var" he suggested.

"I shall call you little Var" said the giant as he pulled up a stool to sit facing the tribesman. Var shrugged his shoulders, it was not like he had a choice.

"Tell me" started Gero, "You are an ocean man I presume, so I am confused as to why I found you on board a Dumon Vehicle with a dead Dumon and dead sea creatures." Var remembered back to the events. They were confusing and he felt a terrible sadness as he thought of Bronsur and Astur.

"How long have I been asleep?" asked Var.

"Two moons" stated Gero.

Var proceeded to tell the giant his story starting with the bait field and the Murmur attack all the way through his encounters with the Eburus and finally how he had surfaced and ended up on the sea craft. The giant listened intently taking everything in, occasionally raising his eyebrows at Var's story.

"You have been busy" said Gero standing and moving the chair. He walked to the table and picked up a cup from which he shook the previous remnants. He poured in a liquid from a stitched skin flask and offered it to Var. Var clasped the massive cup with both hands and swigged the liquid. It was slightly sour but warmed him as it passed down his throat.

"How did you find me? And where are we?" enquired Var.

"I was fishing when I saw a reflection. There isn't usually much of anything in the ocean so I decided to investigate. I found you unconscious on the deck of that craft. I hooked it up and towed it back."

"It's here!" gasped Var.

"It is" answered Gero. "It's moored next to my skif."

"Is that wise?" proffered Var.

"I am not known for my wisdom, but we will see" smiled Gero.

"I am sorry, I didn't mean to offend. I am very grateful for what you have done. I owe you my life. Thank you Gero." Var's words were sincere. The giant fidgeted clearly uncomfortable with the compliment.

"You owe me nothing little Var. After what you have been through I am glad I could help. As for your question on where we are, perhaps we should take a look outside." The two men brushed passed the curtain out into the bright light. The giant spread his arms wide and turned to Var.

"We are on a chain of islands known as Voremerian's Spine at the end of the known world" he declared. They were standing on top of a cliff looking out over the ocean. A series of smaller islands led away into the distance. White foam soared into the air like angelic embers as the waves crashed into the rocky coastline. The roar of the sea was deadened slightly by the brisk and cold wind that buffeted Var's face. To the left of the island Var recognized the metal sea craft. It was tied to an impressive wooden sailing boat, almost twice the length. The cliffs to the right flattened out and descended down to the ocean's edge. There was a thin wedge of sand between the land and the ocean forming a steep beach. The sky was grey and voluminous clouds sped quickly by overhead. To Gero it was the view that greeted him each morning. To Var it was the most magnificent sight he had ever seen. His life underwater seemed dull and insignificant to the vastness and the glory of the world above.

Gero led the smaller man down onto the beach and they talked amicably. Var was in awe of the giant whist he suspected that Gero was grateful for any company. Apart from his solitary roundhouse there were no other signs of life on the island.

"How do you breathe under the water?" Gero asked.

"We use a plant called Velp" replied Var. "It gives off oxygen. We fill containers with it and it acts like a lung, which reminds me - do you have anywhere around the island where the surface bubbles? It might be a sign of the plant."

"Do you intend to go back beneath the waves?" Gero asked. Var noticed a sudden sadness in his words.

"I must find Bron and make sure that my family is safe" explained Var.

"Of course" answered Gero quickly. The giant led Var around the island and they climbed down onto the shore. A rocky finger jutted out into the ocean.

"Out here" shouted Gero pointing towards the white capped waves. "I have often wondered what it was, thousands of tiny bubbles breaking the surface. It must be your Velp." Var looked out, excited. If he could restock and repair his bio-lung he could try to find Bronsur. He knew deep down this was a long shot. He was spools from anywhere and nowhere above the surface held any relation to that below. He turned back suddenly feeling the chill of the wind. As he looked back he could see out behind the island. Stretching out behind in the opposite direction were more islands larger in size than the one they were on. Beyond that he could see a white glare coming from the sea. Gero noticed his bemused look.

"There are several more islands in that direction. The last of them rises way up into the clouds. It is home to the Fortress of Ages, and the glare you can see is the start of the Southern ice sheet." Everything Gero said intrigued Var, but this especially.

"What is the Fortress of Ages?" Gero looked at the smaller man.

"It was my home once" he said sadly.

*

Bor ran as fast as his young legs would carry him. His bare feet sliding through the mud as he approached the shack. He burst in through the door.

"Muyda, Muyda" he managed to pant, desperately trying to catch his breath.

"Calm down young Bor, take a breath" said Set quietly. Muyda put the cooking pot she was holding onto the floor and knelt up to the breathless young boy.

"What is it? Are you OK?" she asked concerned.

"Yes, Yes" he said now excited. "It's just that I have seen…" he gulped again. "I have seen five sea blades leave the harbour. They were full of Reavers."

"Five!" exclaimed Set. "That's a lot. Were they from the fortress or had they come through the gate?"

"Some I didn't recognize" said Bor "But most were from the fortress." Muyda looked up at Set in anticipation. He saw the fire and zeal in her eyes and knew what was coming.

"We'll never get another chance like this" she said. She grabbed the young boy by the arms. "Thank you Bor, now go and prepare."

The driftwood town bristled with activity. After Muyda's recent speech she had been surprised and somewhat overwhelmed by the response. All knew the dangers and the risks, but all were behind it, their hope ignited. Their plan was simple. They would storm the harbour as it was the least protected, cross the adjoining curtain wall and make their way to the gate and destroy it. Without reinforcements the fortress guards would soon be overwhelmed by the masses of the Murai. With over half the fortresses entourage out at sea the plan suddenly looked achievable.

A handful of people entered the harbour area. A lone Reaver was outside the harbourmasters office. He was sitting staring out to sea and oblivious of the group which approached him. He turned startled as the women drew close.

"What are you doing here? This area is off limits to you lot." His rant was swiftly interrupted as Muyda swung a stick, it clacked against his skull. The blow stunned the Reaver more from shock than pain. The group followed suit and rained down multiple blows. The guard fell to his knees covering his head with his hands. The blood lust and pent up anger from the encircling group quickly beat the Reaver to death. Muyda led the group up the stairs and out onto the adjoining wall. She leant over and signalled to Set below. The group crouched down in nervous apprehension awaiting the main force of the Murai. Set came running up the steps, people crowding in behind him. The first group ran along the wall. All being well the bulk of the Murai would make it inside the fortress before the alarm could be raised.

As the first man neared the end of the wall it was looking good until the head of a Reaver appeared as he made his way up the steps. The group continued their charge. The Reaver looked out along the curtain wall and gasped as he saw the oncoming assault. He reached for his nail gun and un-holstered it. Before he could bring it to bear, the leading Murai leapt carrying both of them over the edge and plummeting to the courtyard below. They landed with a thunderous whump, the Reaver's body breaking the fall for the villager. The Reaver's body lay twisted and unnaturally contorted. The Murai rolled clear, both legs broken. The rest of the Murai quickly spread out around the walls of the fortress. Muyda, Set and the bulk of the horde swept down into the courtyard like an angry tide.

Wik-Te was the Missionrai in charge of the Imercian Fortress. He had complained to the big Dominator about taking the majority of his men. Vas-Sem had explained he was on a personal mission for the Emperor and besides clearly outranked the veteran commander, which left him little choice. There were very few problems on the island mainly because Wik-Te ruled the working population with zero tolerance. The constant threat of fear kept them in line. Wik-Te was a meticulous planner, the one reason he had been given the position on Imercia. His excellent management skills kept a near constant stream of food supplies flowing through the Gate to the home world. It was also the reason he had complained to Vas-Sem. He had wanted to be sure he had covered every eventuality. It was this minute attention to details that had led him to call all remaining Reavers to duty.

The noise of the incursion alerted the old warrior and he rushed to the shuttered window. With horror he saw the flood of Murai pouring into his fortress. One of his guards rushed into the courtyard. He made it two steps before a large piece of stone smashed into his cranium, killing him instantly. Wik-Te turned and wound the handle on the wall which screamed out the alarm.

He was already in his Missonrai armour. He flung open a locker and fixed two additional units onto both forearms before flinging a large canister over his back. He snapped a flexible hose hanging down from the canister into the left arm unit. He grabbed a long halberd from the weapon rack as he ran from the room.

As well as his administration qualities, Wik-Te had been a successful warrior in his time. His black and grey hair was tied back neatly in a pony tail. His face showed the signs of age and battle with scars and wrinkles in equal amount. Despite his advancing age he vaulted down the first flight of stairs. Instead of continuing his descent he charged headlong at the shuttered window.

Muyda looked up startled by the crash. She watched as the Missionrai landed in the courtyard, wood and glass debris raining down around him. She looked at Set and yelled.

"We must get to the gate." A large contingent left the courtyard and headed into the warren of tunnels searching for their target.

Wik-Te shook the fragments of glass from his armour. He withdrew his nail gun and with an unwavering outstretched arm aimed and squeezed the trigger. The metal spikes spat out. He continued the onslaught as his arm moved steadily in an arc. Dozens of Murai that had packed in closely fell from the ramparts as if a strong wind had caught them. The shards wreaked havoc in the un-armoured ranks of the Murai.

Two more Reavers bolted into the killing ground alongside the defiant Missionrai. He barked orders at them and they disappeared back inside. Wik-Te had see the group of Murai enter the fortress corridors and knew exactly where they were headed. He had sent the two Reavers back to the gate chamber to seal it. He would have to follow the Murai to ensure they didn't get there first. Before this he had to cross the courtyard which was now blocked by scores of villagers armed with clubs and scavenged weapons.

He threw the empty gun onto the floor and leapt forward. He held the halberd with both hands on the end swinging if before him in a devastating strike. The blade severed heads and tore through flesh as he cleaved it back and forth. The gathered masses shrank before the master warrior's prowess. They withdrew and changed their tactics. Wik-Te now came under a bombardment of stones, sticks and numerous other improvised missiles. He lunged forward with the deadly pole arm skewering a hapless woman who stood between him and the entrance to the corridors. The Murai kept up their tirade from a safe distance, one piece of stone bouncing off the veteran's head. He reached up and felt the warm trickle of blood on his fingers.

Muyda and Set ran through the corridors and came across their first obstacle. The two Reavers who had been ordered to the gate had closed the outer doors. The thick studded wooden door was securely fastened. Muyda stared through the small barred window. She could see the Reavers and beyond that the sparking pillars of the portal gate.

"We're nearly there!" she shouted. "We must get this door opened." A tall man stepped forward with a woodcutter's axe and set to work attacking the hinges. A few sound blows and the door swung away. The assembled Murai held onto the door and walked forward using it as a makeshift shield as the Reavers ahead unleashed their nail guns. Realising the oncoming crowd would soon be in the gate chamber itself they cast each other a quick glance and charged the advancing door. The two warriors rammed into the door knocking it flat and trampling the Murai behind underfoot. They drew their swords and prepared for combat. The two warriors fought bravely but were soon overpowered by numbers as the Murai hacked and stabbed at the two defenders. Muyda looked at the pile of bodies that lay before her. The corridor stank of blood. She looked down at her feet; the blood had trickled along the corridor and had soaked into her thin sandals. She felt the sticky liquid on her toes.

"What have I done Set?" she said looking despairingly at the corpse-laden corridor.

"You have given us a reason to live and more than that our freedom to enjoy it" replied Set placing his hand on her shoulder. Muyda spun, quickly alerted by the sound of grinding stone. The primary door to the gate chamber was a huge stone slab that could be lowered down into the two grooves on either side of the corridor. Gears whined and chains rattled as the monolith slowly lowered.

"Quick!" shouted Set. His impromptu advance was halted swiftly and he slid along the floor desperately trying to back track away from the large warrior that stepped under the closing stone door. Wik-Te wiped the blood from his eyes and then clicked a button on his left arm. A small pilot light sprang to life beneath his arm.

"Run!" cried Muyda. Wik-Te lifted his arm upward as if pointing at the gathered towns people. A huge jet of flame erupted from his arm unit chasing the fleeing Murai down the corridor. As the roar of the first burst of flame subsided the corridor echoed with a resounded thud as the entrance to the gate was sealed.

*

After a hearty breakfast the two men ventured out from the roundhouse and Var immediately noticed the change in the landscape. The ocean had receded and exposed a sandy causeway to the next island. They clambered down the rocks, Var almost running to keep pace with the giant's strides. They crossed the thin sandy corridor and walked up onto the next island. Following a brisk walk they arrived at the far end. Gero sat down on an exposed outcrop of rock staring out over the ocean. Var lifted his head. He had tucked his head into the fur cloak Gero had given him shielding his face from the fierce winds. What he now saw stopped him in his tracks.

On the smaller island out in front were the ruins of an ancient city. The derelict buildings clung to the cliffs and he could make out structures stretching out into the sea. There were huge pillars, some broken, but all now supporting only the sky. On top of the island the buildings were more complete and a single minaret completed the amazing skyline.

"This is, or rather was, the city of Palenique" said Gero.

"It's amazing" replied Var. "We have a ruin near our village which has similar architecture although it is nowhere near as well preserved."

"What do you call the ruin?" queried Gero.

"Coba, we call it Coba." The giant smiled.

"I thought as much" said Gero contently.

"What do you mean?"" asked Var.

"I would also guess it is built on an underwater mountain" suggested Gero.

"Yes it is!" said a surprised Var. "It's built on the top of a seamount."

"They are all that is left of the Magta civilization" started Gero. "In the time before the oceans swallowed the land, my people the Magta were spread far and wide across the planet. We are the oldest of the races that have populated this world. You my little friend are the latest. Your predecessors, however, are the ones that almost destroyed the planet completely. The man on the sea craft and the one you killed are part of that race. They are Dumons. I believe they call themselves Dumonii." Var had always loved tales of history but this was unlike anything he had heard from the Wordkeeper.

"What happened?" Var asked.

"The plague of Dumons spread throughout the land. They built vast cities and populated every corner of available space. We traded and taught them at first but it soon became clear they had no respect for life and their advance would soon overwhelm even our great civilization. They fought between themselves and waged war against each other. It would have only been a matter of time before our ancient cities would have entered into the conflict. One of the great shamans 'Hagon of the Shining Caste' foretold the end of the world. With this prediction we retreated from the world completely. We built new cities on top of Gebshu's mightiest mountains far from the greedy and polluting reach of the Dumon. What you see before you is the remains of one of those cities as is the city of Coba near your home."

"What of my people Gero. Where do the ocean tribes come from? Our Wordkeepers say we descended from Povian the God of the sea. Does this also mean you know where Coba is, because if so I could find my way back?"

"So many questions" sighed Gero still smiling. "Yes I could navigate to Coba. That was the reason I brought you here to see this ruined city. As to where your people came from I wouldn't want to get into a theological debate." Gero stood and started to walk back.

"Gero!" shouted Var. "What about the Fortress of Ages? Is that a ruin? Are you the last of the Magta?" Gero stopped but didn't turn.

"The Fortress of Ages still stands in all its glory. I am the last of the old Magta. The people who live there now have forgotten who they are." Var decided not to push the big man and quietly joined him en route back to the hut. As they neared the causeway the tide had turned and was narrowing the sandy bridge. As they climbed the rocks towards the roundhouse Gero spun around and reached down to Var. Var reached up and grabbed his hand, the giant hauled the smaller man up the rock in one swift and easy movement.

"I will help you find your friends" Gero said suddenly and then turned to stride off towards the hut. Var looked out across the ocean. There was so little he knew about this world and the people that lived within; he felt so small against it, much like how he felt when he stood next to his giant friend. It had been a few moons since the Eburus had taken Bronsur. He prayed he would not be too late.

That afternoon Var made his way out along the rocky outcrop that Gero had shown him earlier that day. With Gero's advice he had wrapped extra animal skin around his legs and arms and done the same beneath his skin. He would need the extra insulation in the colder water. He gingerly stepped into the ocean and the cold water gradually penetrated his wrappings. After several moons spent above the surface huddled around a warm fire the temperature was a shock to the system. Despite the cold Var felt comfortable being back in his natural environment. He swam out towards the bubbling Velp field.

Gero was feeling particularly up beat. He enjoyed the company of his little friend, it had been far too long since he had enjoyed conversation. He was somewhat selfishly looking forward to their forthcoming adventure. A loud hum woke him from his thoughts. He stepped outside and out on the horizon he could see several craft approaching at speed. He looked to the left towards the rocky finger; there was no sign of Var.

Gero fastened his cuirass tightly and hefted his golden axe onto his back as he loped off towards the anchored vessels. It was not long before the sea blades came into view, five in total. One pulled alongside Gero's skif. A tall man in black armour jumped onto the boat and clambered across to the moored sea blade. A few moments later he bounded back. One of the other men had noticed Gero stood alone at the top of a small beach. The sea blades rumbled closer before casting in their anchors. The big man was shouting orders and gesturing at the others. 'He must be the leader' thought Gero.

Vas-Sem had instructed one man to remain aboard each craft. The rest had jumped over the side and were swimming with difficulty towards the shore. Gero stood patiently, his massive axe grasped firmly in both hands. The Reavers came ashore clearly suffering from their short exposure to the icy water. One man drew his side arm and levelled it at Gero. The leader held out his hand to stop him.

"Don't bother with that; it won't work after being submerged" said Vas-Sem. The Reaver reluctantly placed his gun back in its holster and drew his sword. The newly arrived party all unsheathed or un-clicked their various weapons, all except Vas-Sem. He stepped forward towards the giant.

"I am looking for my brother. He was aboard that vessel moored next to that boat" stated Vas-Sem pointing in the direction of Gero's skif. The Giant shrugged his shoulders.

"I wouldn't know anything about that" said Gero jovially.

"Is that your sailing boat?" asked Vas-Sem.

"It is" stated Gero.

"Then I think you know more than you are telling me" said Vas-Sem struggling to keep his composure.

"Then you think too much" retorted Gero as he spat his defiance onto the ground. Vas-Sem was about to give the order to attack but before he could utter a word Gero had grabbed his axe by the blade and swung it outwards. The haft cracked into Vas-Sem's head knocking him out. Gero spun the axe and advanced on the stunned Reavers.

The first Reaver made the mistake of trying to block the giant's axe swing. The massive blade snapped the guard's sword like a twig and thudded into his side almost chopping through his body completely. Gero withdrew the axe and with one hand swung it in a low arc. The giant's reach was enormous and the deadly blades severed the legs of two Reavers just above the ankles, dropping them screaming to the floor. One man saw his opportunity and lashed out with his morning star, the heavy spiked ball slamming into the shoulder of the giant warrior. With lightning reaction Gero reversed his axe and rammed it backwards. The pointed cap shattering the man's armour and puncturing his stomach. He fell backwards clutching the hole in his abdomen leaving his weapon embedded in Gero's shoulder.

The remaining soldiers circled the giant with renewed caution, the blow from the weapon stuck in his shoulder not apparently causing him any pain. Gero leapt forward swinging his axe in a deadly circle, one Reaver leapt back to avoid the blow whilst another ducked beneath it. The crouched man was sent flying backwards as Gero's heel slammed into his chin. The force of the blow snapping his neck.

Gero growled as another blade cut deep into his left arm. He turned and used the flat of the axe to bat down the follow up thrust. The attacking soldier made the mistake of holding on to his weapon. A mistake he realized moments too late as the twin prongs of the golden axe entered his chest. Gero swung the axe flinging the dead man into his companions, spraying the entire scene with his crimson blood. He advanced quickly on the stumbling men, a one handed upward blow cleanly decapitating a fleeing warrior. His headless body seemed to stagger surprised at the loss before collapsing into the sand. Gero grabbed the handle with both hands and wheeled it overhead. The blood stained blades smashed through the shoulder plate cleaving deep into the warrior's chest. Gero tried to pull the axe free but his first attempt was thwarted as the blades' prongs snagged on the dead man's ribcage. As he attempted a second pull his vision swam as he felt a heavy blow hammer into the back of his head. The giant slumped to the ground. Vas-Sem unleashed his war hammer a second time knocking Gero unconscious.

Var surfaced, his net bulging with Velpaynix. He swam for the short distance to the shore and as he climbed from the ocean he saw the dark plume of smoke billowing into the air. He raced along the beach, dropping his catch as he went. He leaped up the rocky path and ran along the edge of the cliff. As he stood overlooking the small bay he could see Gero's skif half submerged and the remainder ablaze. Out beyond he could make out six vessels skimming the surface of the ocean quickly fading away into the distance. Down to his left he saw the bloody corpse strewn beach.

Var vaulted down the rock face, his heart pounding and his mind racing. There were the remains of eight bodies scattered across the blood soaked sand. Var grimaced at the sight of the dismembered and shattered bodies. To his relief there was no sign of his friend. Two large grooves in the sand led down to the water's edge and Var realized his newly acquired companion had been taken. He put his hands to his head and fell to his knees feeling overwhelming guilt.

"Why!" he cried out.

*

Time passed slowly and Var remained motionless, kneeling in the sand. The cold wash of the ocean stirred him. He stood a determined look on his face.

"I'm not done yet" he said to himself. He removed two belts from the fallen warriors and slung them around the blades of Gero's golden axe and strapped it to his back. The huge weapon hung only a boot's length from the ground. Var set off at a steady pace. He climbed the winding path out across the back of the island. The bigger islands and that of the Fortress of Ages lay ahead. Var waded into the ocean and was soon racing across the second island. The main island beyond was a lengthy swim across a turbulent stretch of ocean which would be made more difficult by the weight of the axe. Despite the difficulties Var made short work of the dividing sea. As he approached the mainland he could see an enormous stone pier projecting into the water. Var reached it and climbed a wooden ladder; he continued to walk along the top of the massive structure. There were several large sailing boats moored against the pier similar in design to Gero's but there was no sign of anyone. Var continued and came to a well worn cobbled track that led up the hill and disappeared a short distance away into the mist.

After a long hike Var finally stood before the magnificent gates of the Fortress of Ages. Two huge statues carved from stone stood guarding the entrance. The two goliaths were modelled in the image of their creators, standing twenty times the height of Var, their arms folded, bearded and with circular shields at their feet. The walls of the vast citadel stretched out to either side blurring into the distance. A crenellated bridge spanned the distance between the two statues, finishing the impressive gateway. Two wooden doors with metal braces wrought in the shapes of various mythical beasts stood open and Var could see the busy city scene inside. He walked forward staring up open mouthed at the giant gate. A nearby woman, just as large as Gero but with a patterned scarf covering her head gave him an unconcerned glance.

The city was constructed in tiers and between each level were the houses, workshops, traders and taverns of the Magta. Stretching out from the sky scraping walls were large canopies. The canopies protected the streets below from the elements whilst also casting a gloomy shadow. The location of the great fortress had given its occupants the remoteness they required but its proximity to the southern ice sheet meant that it was harried by cold winds and regular snow fall. The crisp white snow still remained on the tops of the walls and across the canopies. There were small smatterings in the street but this snow was grey and dirty.

An exceptionally large man approached the bewildered Var, his fur cloak flowing out behind him. He was dressed in a similar fashion to Gero although his breast plate was un-dented and highly polished.

"Are you lost little man?" said the giant, and he frowned as he noticed the load on the small man's back.

"I am looking for someone in authority" replied Var with confidence. "I am a friend of Gero."

"Is that his axe?" asked the giant guard.

"Yes it is. I have come here seeking help" stated Var. The big man raised his eyebrows and chuckled.

"Follow me." The giant turned and Var raced after him. They entered the second level of the citadel and the busy Magta turned their heads and stared at the ocean tribesman as he sped after his guide. They approached an impressive and official looking building. The façade was supported by gigantic pillars and two huge statues of crouching menvhir guarded the stepped approach. They climbed the stone steps and entered the regal building. The inside was no less impressive. Huge arches soared overhead, intricate carving covering every available space. The black marble floor reflected the magnificence of the ceiling. They stood at the start of a long corridor with doors leading off to either side. The giant continued straight on towards two gleaming golden doors at the end of the walkway. He flung them open and the gathered throng inside stopped their conversation and turned their attention to the unlikely pair of newcomers.

The chamber was not as large as Var had imagined after the grand entrance. On either side there were wooden seats which were staggered in height, at the end of the room was a man sitting alone on a simple stone bench. All were dressed in furs and watched with intrigue as Var approached the seated monarch.

"My Lord, this man is a friend of Gero. He has asked to speak to someone in authority concerning assistance." The man smiled at Var and gestured to him to proceed. The seated giant stood.

"I am Titan Lothair. With whom am I speaking?" Var remembered Gero's musing at his initial formal introduction.

"I am Var, I am from the ocean people of the Enki."

"What can I do for you little man?" said Lothair.

"I am friends with one of your people – Gero. He saved my life, but I am afraid my actions may now have endangered his life." The assembly remained silent. Var looked around the gathered Magta searching for a reaction. He saw no sign of emotion, and so cleared his throat.

"I believe the Dumon have taken him. I came here to ask for help in rescuing him." Titan Lothair stared in amused disbelief at Var. He threw his head back and laughed. The rest of the entourage joined in the chorus of laughter.

"Little man" started Lothair. "I admire your loyalty to your friend, but I am afraid Gero is not a friend of this court. He is no longer regarded as a Magta; he is an outcaste. I am surprised he didn't tell you. Besides, it is not the concern of the Magta to get involved with the treacherous Dumon." It was Var's turn to stare in disbelief.

"Is that it?" shouted Var. "Gero told me you had forgotten who you were. He is one of you despite whatever it is he has done and he needs your help" pleaded Var. Titan Lothair stepped down to confront the smaller man

"Do not come into my house and challenge me dwarf" he barked. "Gero left this city and its people behind. He is outcaste and so is dead to us already and has been for many seasons."

"Well I have only known him for a few moons and he was prepared to help me look for my lost friends. I had hoped his good grace was a common trait amongst his people. I can see now why you cower from the world outside these walls." Var looked up into the furious eyes of the Titan. The guide that had shown Var in stepped in shepherding him away.

"Time to leave" he said sternly as he led him to the door.

"You know your way out. I suggest you don't show your face here again" and he slammed the door. Var couldn't believe it. These were once a great people who had survived the great flood. They may as well not exist he thought. The door to the great building opened again and an old man appeared in the doorway.

"I know someone who may help you" he said simply. Var followed the old giant back out through the fortress gateway and back down to the harbour. He accompanied the old man to a roundhouse similar in construction to Gero's.

"Wait here" he said and entered the building. A while later he emerged escorted by an even older man. His beard was ice white and his face wrinkled and weathered. He stooped slightly and supported himself with a walking stick. He was dressed completely in grey fur, a grey hat topping out his outfit. The two giants shook hands and the first man hurried away.

"So" croaked the old giant. "You called our beloved Titan a coward." He moved towards Var and spun him around to view the axe on his back.

"Well" started Var.

"Quiet boy" shouted the old man. "It wasn't a question. How long ago was your friend taken?" asked the giant.

"The tide had just crossed the sand bridge" replied Var.

"Hmmm" said the old man stroking his white beard. "What will you do if we find him?" asked the old man. Var looked into the man's eyes and held his questioning gaze.

"I will do whatever I can" said Var.

"Good enough" declared the giant. "Come we don't have much time, we must catch the winds if we are to track down these Dumon devils." Var didn't understand, perhaps the old man knew someone else who would help. His look of confusion was easy to read.

"What?" snapped the old man. "Do you think I am too old to pilot a sailboat?"

"Eh, no" stuttered Var.

"I should hope not" muttered the old giant. "I am the best sea pilot there is. I have forgotten more than you'll ever learn about navigating this world's oceans."

"I didn't mean to question your ability" placated Var. The old man sniffed.

"Do as I tell you and we'll have no problems. My name is Hanelore." Var offered his hand in friendship but the giant turned his back and walked toward the harbour.

"Get my bag little man, it's just inside the door."

Chapter 6 – Dead End

It had been several rotations since Ty-Sem and the squad of Reavers had arrived at Morlok-Tun. They had taken up residence in a small barrack room next to the southern entrance to the town. It was comfortable but the six men hadn't planned on spending any time at all in the dusty outpost and were beginning to get restless. Gen-Su was a veteran Reaver, he had been excited by the prospect of action but this waiting game was not what he had signed up for. He was making his thoughts known to the rest of the squad.

"This was supposed to be an emergency deployment" complained Gen-Su. "We have been here for two rotations already and there is no sign of Bok or his moody brother. Whatever the problem was it is sure to have passed by now. I just wish we could get out of this dust trap and see some action." At that moment the formidable figure of Ty-Sem entered the room. He had overheard the squad's conversation.

"Careful what you wish for Gen. The last squad they sent out never made it back" stated Ty-Sem.

"Surely that's even more reason to get going, they might still be alive" suggested Gen-Su.

"I agree" sighed Ty-Sem. "I have been down to the garage and spoken with the replicator. A grounder is ready

145

and waiting for us." The squad looked excited, eager to be on their way.

"What about Bok and his brother?" asked Per-Su. "Wasn't his brother supposed to be in charge of this mission?" Ty-Sem turned on the young Reaver.

"Watch your mouth boy" said the Dominator through gritted teeth. The young soldier shrank away from the older man.

"The way I see it" started Ty-Sem. "Is that we are on the Emperor's mission. He would want this issue brought to a swift conclusion. He may already be wondering why we are not reporting back. For all we know Vas and Bok may have been re-assigned. I have learnt from painful experience it is not wise to keep Lord Senn waiting. We will leave mission and route details with the replicator here, so they can catch up if they do arrive." The squad seemed perfectly happy with Ty-Sem's reasoning and set about stowing their equipment and preparing for the mission in the deep desert.

The squad entered the garage and saw a grounder in each of the two repair bays. Both looked like they had seen better days. The Grounder MkIII was the main personnel transport vehicle used by the Dumonii. It was effectively an armoured box. It had a sloping front with a small slit for the driver and was propelled along by metal caterpillar tracks on either side. Two large exhausts rose vertically out from the rear. A large door which was hinged on the bottom allowed access for men and equipment to the cramped rear space. On top there was an armoured circular mounting platform to which a hefty nail gun was attached. The vehicle was painted in desert livery and had the Emperor's star emblem across the front and sides. The emblems like most of the paint was flaking away and judging by the amount of dust on all the surfaces it hadn't been cleaned since its last outing.

A small rotund replicator appeared from the rear of the garage, a large wrench in his hands. He looked up warily at Ty-Sem and his squad.

"It's all ready. You should have plenty of fuel for the return journey and the nail gun has been completely overhauled."

"It looks like a heap" said Gen-Su. "The other one looks in better condition" and he pointed to the other vehicle.

"Does it really? Well that one doesn't have an engine" smirked the replicator.

"Well you could have at least cleaned this one" retorted Gen-Su. The small man turned to the vehicle, huffed on the sleeve of his jerkin and used it to clean a light lens on the back of the grounder. Gen-Su jumped into the bay and drew his firearm and rammed it against the head of the replicator.

"Make fun of me now you greasy rep!" threatened Gen-Su.

"Put that away!" shouted Ty-Sem. "Their primary vehicle never made it back from the last outing; we are lucky we are not walking there." Gen-Su sheathed his gun all the while glaring at the nonchalant replicator. The squad piled into the rear of the vehicle and stowed their gear beneath the basic seats. Per-Su climbed through and squeezed himself into the driver's seat; Ty-Sem sat next to him. He used his fingers to wipe the dust from the periscope viewing screen and pushed his face against the soft surround. It gave him a clear view of the garage interior.

"Start this bucket up and let's get going" commanded Ty-Sem. The last man in pulled the heavy ramp door shut. With the door closed the light disappeared. Now the only light came from the thin window slits. As the engine grumbled awake a small interior light flickered on. It had a red lens and cast an eerie glow over the confined men.

Per-Su was used to the controls of the antique grounder and in a short time the town of Morlok-Tun was well behind them.

Apart from the few rivers and lakes scattered around Son-Gebshu the majority of the moon was mountainous or desert. These outer regions were also bombarded by dust storms, some that lasted for rotations.

The small vehicle thundered along the dusty road creating a small brown cloud of its own behind it. The men in the back were lost in their own thoughts, preparing themselves for whatever lay ahead, the gentle hum of the engine and tracks gently rocking them asleep. Per-Su stamped on the brakes sending the dozing squad flying into each other. Ty-Sem steadied himself against the interior.

"What is it?" he asked.

"Not sure" replied Per-Su. The following dust cloud had now caught up with them enveloping the vehicle and reducing visibility to zero. "It looked like a break in the track."

"Open the door and let's have a look" said Ty-Sem. The rear door thumped into the road and the squad disembarked the grounder. They drew their weapons and proceeded cautiously along the track, Gen-Su taking the point. He slowly faded from view in the dust cloud.

"Whoa!" came the reaction through the haze. As the sand and dust settled they could see Gen-Su standing at the edge of a sheer drop. There was a narrow canyon which cut straight across the track way. On either side were stone emplacements and the remains of arched buttresses sticking out from either side. They were remnants of an ancient bridge which had obviously given way.

"That was close!" exclaimed one of the Reavers.

"Mount up" barked Ty-Sem. "We'll have to find another way around." The vehicle swivelled on its tracks and made its way back down the road. Per-Su yanked on the control levers and the personnel carrier lurched to the left and off the track. The terrain was bumpy but the grounder had no problem traversing the desert landscape. They entered a shallow canyon which resembled a dried up riverbed. Per-Su opened the throttle and the vehicle sped along the reasonably flat surface.

The vehicle was suddenly rocked by a huge explosion lurching it to one side. The motor died and with it the internal lighting dimmed. There were groans from the men and complete confusion as to what had just happened. Ty-Sem coughed as he raised himself off the floor.

"What the depths was that?" he exclaimed. "Per can you get it started?" There was no answer. Ty-Sem reached out for the driver; he could make out his outline slumped over the driving controls. He felt for a pulse in his neck but quickly retracted his hand as he felt the warm sticky blood coating the dead driver's neck. The explosion had shattered one of the tracks and had detonated beneath the driver's seat sending shrapnel into the cabin killing Per-Su. There were coughs and curses from the surviving men.

"Sound off" commanded Ty-Sem. Each of the four men shouted out their names. "Is anyone hurt?" asked the Dominator.

"Only cuts and bruises" replied Gen-Su. "Is Per OK?"

"He's dead" replied Ty-Sem calmly. He moved the dead body back in the seat and reached across to the ignition. The engine turned but did not start. After several attempts the big man gave up. He grabbed the handles of the periscope and stared closely at the screen. There were no signs of life. Smoke started to creep into the confined space.

"Gen, get on that mount and give us some cover, the rest of you will come with me. We'll make a sprint for the eastern bank. I can't see anything outside but I'm taking no chances. Gen-Su wound the handle to the hatch and hauled himself up through the opening. A series of shrill sounds rang out, metal on metal, peppering the hull of the vehicle. Gen-Su groaned and fell back into the cabin. Two large spikes jutting from his chest and neck. The shards were from a large calibre weapon which meant they had been fired from a mounted position. Gen-Su tried to speak but blood bubbled from his mouth and he sank back, his eyes rolling in his head.

"Not good" gasped Fo-Su.

"This is a set up" growled Ty-Sem. "Curse that Vas-Sem."

"Do you think it's him out there?" asked Fo-Su.

"I don't think he would be stupid enough to get his hands dirty, but you can bet he was behind it. Why else do you think the Emperor's two sons couldn't join us" he barked.

"What do we do now?" asked Fo-Su panic starting to creep in as they realized the seriousness of the situation.

"We can stay in here and burn to death" said Ty-Sem. "Or we can attempt to make it out and take some of these nameless cowards with us." They dropped the rear door which seemed to the condemned men to fall in slow motion. One by one they bolted out of the vehicle. They didn't stand a chance. Despite their ceramic armour the guns from the hidden figures on either side of the old river bed caught them in a devastating cross fire. The squad only made it a few lengths from the grounder before falling headlong into the dust.

Ty-Sem fell heavily on his face. He felt the pain of multiple metal spikes buried deep in his flesh. He could hear shouting and then footsteps as the ambushers approached. He felt an arm on his shoulder as the attacker attempted to roll him over. As he did Ty-Sem brought up his nail gun and squeezed the trigger. The gun emptied its deadly load in the face of his enemy. The dead body fell on top of Ty-Sem. He groaned as the fingers on his hand were wrenched apart and the gun removed. The dead body on top of him was moved away and a young Reaver stood over him looking at him with utter contempt.

"Why?" gurgled Ty-Sem his lungs filling with blood.

"You are a traitor and the Emperor wants you dead" said the man. He raised his arm and pulled the trigger. A single shot thudded into the temple of the dying Dominator.

"Gather the bodies and pile them in the vehicle" commanded the man. "Burn everything. There must be nothing left."

*

Var hauled the old man's belongings onto the sailboat. Despite his apparent old age and his walking stick, the ageing giant clambered around the boat like an eager youth.

"Untie the ropes fore and aft" shouted Hanelore. Var ran along the pier and unwrapped the heavy rope from the rusty metal hoop. He threw it onto the ship and then did the same thing with the other retaining rope. He jumped aboard the boat and awaited his next task.

The vast ship consisted of a long and slender central hull and on either side two equally long outriggers connected to the central vessel by two beautifully curved beams. It was magnificently crafted from timber that fitted together seamlessly. The sailboat had three massive masts, two on either edge of the central hull and one a few lengths in from the prow. Hanelore was stood aft of the boat where the wheel and cabin were located. He had asked Var to take hold of some handles. There were two seats each with handles set in front. Hanelore joined the tribesman in the adjacent seat grabbing hold of the handles and started to rotate them. Var copied his actions and to his surprise the handles spun with ease.

The handles were attached to a complicated gearing system. The simple hand rotations were magnified many times and the power was eventually transferred to two colossal water screws beneath the hull. As the screws turned in the water the giant vessel moved forward gracefully. Var was amazed that such little effort could move the huge sailboat with ease. Within moments they were clear of the harbour and moving past the string of islands.

"Tell me about their sea craft?" said the old man.

"They had small wings with fans in them" said Var. "They seemed to float on top of the water. I think there were six of them."

"Hmmm" said Hanelore again stroking his beard as was his habit. "What side of the island did they leave on?" he asked.

"On the side we are on now" replied Var. "Do you know where they are headed?"

"Of course I do boy" said the old man. "I just needed to be sure which of the two islands they would head for. Now stop all your questioning and set to that winch." He pointed at a large handle attached to a rope wound drum. He wound the handle and the large boom attached to the mast swung out over his head and a linen sail started to unfold. Hanelore was doing the same thing on the opposite side of the boat. The two enormous sails billowed in the wind and Var felt the push as the strong winds caught the sails. Hanelore moved to the front of the vessel and unwound a third sail before returning to the wheel.

Var stood on the prow of the sail boat as the mammoth craft scythed through the water. Its speed was incredible. He had been amazed at the mechanical sea blades but they were mere toys in comparison to the sail boat of the Magta. Var revelled in the speed, the wind blowing his hair out behind him. He felt sure they would catch up with Gero but he wasn't so sure what they would do when they did.

Var re-joined the old man at the stern. He was studying a strange circular device. A pointer danced across the surface. Hanelore moved an outer bezel and then squinted again at the pointing device.

"Does that tell us where we are going?" quizzed Var.

"I tell us where we are going, that's all you need to know" grumbled Hanelore. Var chuckled. He liked the cantankerous old man despite his best efforts to the contrary.

"Why did you help me?" asked Var.

"Who says I did" mumbled Hanelore. "Maybe I was heading this way anyway and you are just along for the ride."

"You're helping Gero aren't you?" suggested Var.

"Pah" spat the old man. "That boy has been nothing but trouble since he was your age. I am afraid that he takes after his father, he was a foolish old grote."

"Is his father dead?" asked Var.

"As good as" said the old man. "Now get in that cabin and fix me a hot drink."

The journey continued well; the strong winds remained in their favour and Var baited the old sailor with more questions. As the light faded, Var yawned and drew the short sword he had found on board the Dumon sea vessel. He marvelled at the strange symbols along its blade. It was exquisite craftsmanship and had a razor sharp edge. He thumbed the blade idly and it drew a thin red line across his thumb.

"That's a Dumon blade" interrupted the old man.

"I got it on the sea plane" said Var.

"It's a bad omen, you should throw it into the depths" suggested Hanelore.

"It just seems too good a weapon to throw away. Anyway what is it about the Dumon that all you Magta are afraid of?"

"Afraid!" exclaimed Hanelore. "The Magta are not afraid of the Dumon little man. It is just the nature of all things. We ruled this planet for millennia. Our time ended when the Dumon arrived. We were not afraid, we were simply resigned to the will of the gods and the planet. We were a dying people then and I am surprised we have made it this long."

"You could have fought them though" asked Var. "Despite their numbers. Gero killed eight of them single handed."

"Only eight, he must be getting old" laughed the old giant. "The Dumon had their time in ascendency as did we, but unlike us they still believe this is the case. The world is in transition and only the gods know what will happen." The old man tapped the directional device with his finger.

"We could have fought I suppose, that is true. I think it would have served little purpose. Perhaps it would have ended our dynasty, or perhaps it would have started a new one. Who knows? You have met our illustrious Titan Lothair and you have seen firsthand how much interest he has in the rest of the world."

"He is a fool" uttered Var angry at the memory of the Magta leader. Hanelore laughed.

"Gero is not like that" said Var. "And neither are you. Perhaps there is still hope for a new Magta dynasty."

"I do so love the exuberance of youth" smiled the old man. "Quick pass me that tube." Var bent down and passed the device he was pointing at. Hanelore placed the tube to his eye and then smiled at Var.

"They're in our sights boy. Drop the front sail we don't want to get too close."

*

Gero lay on the deck of the sea blade, heavy manacles around his wrists and ankles. His head pounded from the hammer blows and his body ached from the lack of practice. It had been many seasons since he bore his axe in anger. He coughed, trying to dislodge the cloth that was stuffed into his mouth. It had been put there by his captors to stop his taunts.

Vas-Sem was in the cabin staring across the ocean. He knew his actions had been reckless and his father would be angry, but despite his brother's scant regards for the rules he had felt compelled to search for him. He had no doubt he was dead and the freak he had captured would tell him everything he wanted to know when they reached Imercia. He turned to look at his prisoner. He despised this world and everything in it, especially their reliance on it.

The light of a new morning was filtering its way across the ocean. Vas-Sem could see the island of Imercia on the horizon. After a short time the fleet of sea blades made their way slowly into the harbour. One of his men jumped onto the jetty and set about mooring the vessel. They heard a high pitch wine and then jumped as the harbour defence nail gun opened up. The force of the shots knocked the disembarked man from his feet. The shots continued to rain down across the boats, breaking glass and splintering wood.

"Take cover" yelled Vas-Sem. He looked carefully out from the cabin and could see several bodies on top of the harbourmaster's building.

"Great Gods!" gasped one of the Reavers. "What if they have taken the gate?"

"Then this is your new home" shouted Vas-Sem. "Now let's take this fight to them, they are only the nameless. Give me some cover." The men in the sea blades returned fire and Vas-Sem and a few others ran along the jetty under the covering fire and dived through the windows of the first floor office. The rest of the men attempted the same run, but without the covering shots the gun on the ramparts opened up again, mowing down the helpless Reavers. Four more made it to the safety of the office.

"What about the giant?" asked one man. In the melee Vas-Sem had completely forgotten about his prisoner.

"We can't risk him escaping. Go back and put a bolt through his head" commanded the Dominator. "We'll get to the gun and that should give you some time."

The small group gingerly climbed the stairs. They knew the Murai would be waiting at the top so they carried two tables between them. They approached the top and then leapt out on the flat roof. They ducked behind their makeshift shields as spikes thunked into them. They crouched over the top and returned fire easily picking off the unprotected villagers. Vas-Sem ran towards the terrified young boy who had operated the mounted nail gun. He tried to run as he saw the big Dominator charge but his little legs were no match for the long strides of Vas-Sem and the big man swiped a backfist at the boy. The blow sent him flying over the battlements.

"Get to the giant" bellowed Vas-Sem to the waiting Reaver below.

*

The burns on Set's hands still stung. He cursed at the charred body of Wik-Te that lay blackened and disfigured in the corridor. Set had avoided the initial blast of the flame thrower and the veteran Missionrai had ignored the skeletal figure in his zeal to chase the remainder of the Murai out of the corridor. Set had chased the warrior and launched himself onto his back stabbing down furiously into Wik-Te's neck and shoulders. The big warrior managed to throw Set clear but not before he had hit home with several blows, the last puncturing the fuel cylinder.

Fuel erupted from Wik-Te's back pack covering the walls, floors and the warrior, in the pungent flammable liquid. He pointed the nozzle at Set and opened fire. Set had shielded his face with his arms in an attempt to hide from the fiery blast. The flames licked at his arms blistering the skin. The pain was short lived as the fuel vapour surrounding the Missionrai ignited and he screamed as he disappeared into a ball of flame.

They had lost too many people despite the reduced numbers of guards. They had all been on duty and none had given in quietly, all choosing to fight to the death. The Murai now controlled the fortress but the price had been great. All would still be in vain if they could not get the stone door open. Muyda prayed that no-one had made it through to report on the rebellion. They had to smash through the door before the guards on the sea blades returned. The news that Muyda had been dreading came to her via a runner and she had ordered some of the Murai to man the harbour defences. The news that they had returned and there was heavy fighting did nothing for her confidence. The Murai had picks and hammers and had been relentlessly hammering the monolithic door. Their persistence had paid off and a small hole to one side of the door had appeared. The remaining Murai took it in turns attacking the stone door chipping it away bit by bit. Muyda ordered the remainder of the Murai to the courtyard to help defend the entrance to the corridor at all costs.

*

The lone Reaver darted along the jetty and leapt aboard the sea blade. He stood over the prostrate giant. He unsheathed his gun and aimed it at the giant. Gero glared his defiance at the small man. Gero squinted as a spear point ruptured the Reaver's throat, spraying blood onto the giant. The dying man reached for the spear point in utter surprise and collapsed to the deck. Behind him stood a painfully thin woman holding a serrated knife in her hands. She climbed aboard and removed Gero's gag.

"Thank you young lady" said Gero. The young woman eyed the giant cautiously.

"Why are you in chains?" she asked.

"They didn't take too kindly to me killing their friends" smiled Gero. The wide grin from the big man relaxed the woman.

"Where are the keys?" she asked.

"I think that man out on the jetty had them" said Gero as he nodded in the direction of a dead body. The woman returned and unlocked the giant. He sat up rubbing his wrists and ankles.

"I owe you my life" said Gero. "What is your name?"

"My name is Lot" said the thin woman. "Will you help us?" she asked.

"What do you need?" replied Gero.

"We are trying to break through a stone door."

"It's the least I can do" said Gero standing. The woman was shocked by the size of the giant as he loomed over her. Then he started laughing.

"You're too late" said Gero. "I have already been rescued." Lot looked puzzled. The giant placed a massive hand on her shoulder and turned her around. Stood on the jetty was a youthful looking man with long hair and strange striped markings on his arms and legs.

"How did you get here?" Gero asked. Var turned and pointed to the ageing giant making his way slowly up the jetty with his walking stick.

"I believe you know Hanelore" said Var smiling. Gero climbing onto the jetty and gave Var a hefty slap on the back almost winding him. He turned to the old man and embraced him.

"Thank you father" said Gero.

"Get off me you big oaf. Always in trouble" mumbled Hanelore. "Isn't it about time you mended your ways" lectured the old man.

"I will if you will" complained Gero.

163

"We must go" interrupted Lot.

"Yes of course" said Gero. "Father, wait here with the boat. I have promised to help these people."

"I'm not staying behind to watch the boat. That's a job for an old man" said Hanelore. Gero raised his eyebrows and knew debate would be futile.

"Well just make sure you don't trip me up with that walking stick, you old fool" joked Gero. He looked down at Var.

"What are we waiting for; let's go!" shouted Var.

*

Vas-Sem and the three remaining Reavers raced along the curtain wall. As they neared the end Vas-Sem could see the mass of bodies guarding the entrance to the corridors and hear the feint chink of hammer blows.

"The doors are still closed" he said to himself.

"There's still time" he said turning to the depleted squad. "We have to get to the gate, we will use the service entrance." They nodded their understanding. The small group came out on the fortress walls. They were quickly spotted by the Murai and they started to pelt the warriors with all available missiles. One young woman had retrieved a nail gun and had opened fire. The metal spikes thunked into the legs of one of the Reavers and he

164

toppled into the courtyard. Both stairways down were blocked.

Vas-Sem drew his war hammer from his back and leapt from the parapet. He landed and rolled and as he rose he thundered the hammer upwards into the woman's face splintering her jaw. The Reavers followed suit and the three men ran into the building attempting to access the second unguarded entrance to the gate. As they got inside Vas-Sem turned to the two men.

"I have got to get word to the Emperor at all costs. It is now up to you to guard this entrance. Let no-one pass." The guards both saluted proudly.

"By the Emperor's will."

Vas-Sem continued down the corridor and came face to face with a stone doorway, the exact replica of what the Murai were attacking at the primary entrance. He could hear their voices and the breaking of stone on the other side of the door. He pushed a stone panel on the wall which had looked like just another stone brick, it retracted revealing a combination lock. The lock consisted of ten metal tumblers. He quickly started turning the wheels and with the sequence entered he pulled at the lever. Nothing happened. He swore under his breath as the sound of battle came down the corridor. The two Reavers fought to keep the tide of the Murai at bay.

Vas-Sem scanned the numbers and then altered two of the tumblers and tried again. This time the lever moved, the gears whined and the colossal door started to lift. He jumbled the combination and then crawled beneath the rising door. As soon as he was inside he ran to the door lever and yanked it hard. The opening door halted, the gears whirred and it quickly resealed the room.

*

Gero, Var and Lot arrived at the door and as Lot explained the surprising presence of the two strangers, Gero picked up a sledge hammer and was proceeding to beat the stone door. The power of the blows quickly enlarged the hole; a few well placed strikes and the giant door finally gave in as it cracked across its width. Gero and Var lent into the top half of the door pushing it inwards. The Murai squeezed in to lend a hand and the giant slab slipped inwards and crashed to the floor before toppling over sending up a huge cloud of dust.

"We must destroy the gate" yelled Muyda. Var was the first to climb the broken door. He landed and looked up to see a man in black armour similar to the one he had drowned. He stood next to the shimmering portal. Var drew his short sword and noticed the look of shock on the man's face. Var drew his knife with his other hand and launched it at the armoured soldier.

Vas-Sem side stepped into the portal and disappeared. The knife bounced harmlessly off one of the glowing pillars. He walked across to pick it up. Gero entered the chamber followed by Muyda and Set.

"We just have to break one of the glass-like centres" said Muyda pointing towards the nearest sparking pillar. Gero turned to see Hanelore climbing awkwardly over the broken door dragging a huge golden axe with him.

"Thought you may need this" smiled the old man. Gero grabbed the axe and swung it at the pillar. It chinked into the central core and the white gate flexed. The pillars sparked erratically and the glimmering portal started to pulse. Gero's second strike shattered the Lexan core but not before a gauntleted hand reached out from the void grabbing Var by the hair and jerking him back through it. With a loud pop the gateway flickered and vanished.

Chapter 7 – The Trial

Bronsur was thrown headlong into the cell. She put her hands out to break her fall and she heard the cell door slam behind her.

"You'll rot here like the others if you don't learn your lesson" said the angry jailer. She reached up to her face and felt the bruising around her right eye. It had completely closed over and the pain of the blow was still present, which made her head throb. It had been worth it.

She had been led into the Eburus nest with the rest of the Enki prisoners. The nest was at least twice the size of the communal one in her home pod. Perhaps that was because they were in the capital city of the Eburus – Symerna. They were all bound together at the feet and the scarred women had huddled together for protection. What appeared to be the leader entered the nest and had given them a speech designed to placate them, to encourage them to forget their violent abduction and make a new life for themselves here in their new home. He had explained how the female population of the Eburus tribes had nearly all died with a similar mysterious disease. They had been brought here to ensure the survival and prosperity of the tribe.

As harmless and idyllic as this sounded, the women knew exactly what it meant. Did these men actually believe they would forget what had happened to them and their men folk? They would be in for a big surprise.

The women were divided up and Bronsur had been taken by two guards and delivered to a pod on the outskirts of the city. As she entered the pool a young and older man helped her into the pod. The pods were almost identical to those of the Enki. The two men led her through into the main living room; Bronsur had decided to see how they would treat her before she made a move. The older man left and the young man guided her through into what looked like his sleeping chamber. He gestured for her to sit on a single bed whilst he sat opposite on another. He was young; perhaps only about nineteen seasons. He was plain looking with dark hair and thick eyebrows.

"My name is Raklim. Please have a seat." He was well spoken and seemed to have manners as well as an education. Bronsur sat down opposite the young the man.

"Do you have a name?" he asked quietly.

"Of course I have a name" blurted Bronsur. "I am Bronsur Aon-Vieto Bay-Enki." She emphasised her tribal name with purpose. The young man seemed nervous.

"Firstly I'd like you to know that I had nothing to do with what happened. I was against the move from the start as was my father. It has been a difficult few seasons since our women took sick. Some of us wanted to simply meet with other tribes, tell them our problems and ask for help. Our Helmsman is far too proud and would not agree."

"So instead you murder our men, abduct us, and expect us to give ourselves over to you? Are you insane? Did you not also think that whatever has been killing your women may now kill us also?" The truth of Bronsur's words stung the young man and she could see how he was struggling with the situation.

"Look" said Bronsur. "You seem like a nice person, but I will choose my own future and who I spend it with. I cannot forgive you for what has happened and even though you didn't physically commit the atrocities, you also did nothing to stop them. The man I love will be looking for me and rest assured you don't want to be here when he finds me. You may as well just take me back to the others."

Raklim looked sad and somewhat afraid. He knew what she had said was true and that this had been a stupid idea. If it wasn't for his father he would not have been involved at all.

"Okay" he sighed. "I'll talk to my father and get you taken back." He got up and left the room. He was gone for some time and Bronsur could hear raised voices and then a crash. She debated making a run for it. Just then Raklim's father stormed into the room.

"My son says you won't co-operate" he demanded.

"That's right" declared Bronsur.

"Then maybe you will for me" he growled as he threw himself at shocked woman. The weight of the man pushed her back onto the bed and he held her hands and attempted to kiss her neck. As he did Bronsur sunk her teeth into his ear as hard as she could. The man screamed and pulled away. He lashed out with his hand smacking Bronsur in the face. She kicked out in return catching him in the groin. He doubled over with pain. Bronsur scrabbled on the bedside table and grabbed a clay bowl which she slammed down over the man's head.

Raklim appeared at the door to see his father lying groaning on the floor, blood matting in his hair.

"I'm sorry" he said.

"One day you'll know what it is to be a real man" said Bronsur. The look on his face was more than just an apology for his father and she noticed his skin was freshly wet. An Eburus guard appeared behind him.

"Come with me whore" demanded the soldier. Bronsur stood and as she passed the young man she whispered.

"You will be judged by your actions one day soon."

Bronsur looked around the circular prison. It was a large pod and had small cells on two levels all around it. It looked like it had been recently converted for this purpose as normally tribes didn't require prisons. Justice was swift and final for anyone who broke the rules. She felt proud to

171

see that all of the cells were full of other Enki women, some in a worse state then she was but all remained defiant. She thought of the women that weren't here and what horrors they might be enduring. She curled up in a ball trying to keep warm and closed her eyes. This time her thoughts turned to Var and she prayed he was still alive.

*

Vas-Sem held the tribesman firmly by the throat pinning him against the wall. He punched Var in the stomach and let him sag to the floor. Var groaned with the beating. Vas-Sem yanked the young man's head back by his hair and held the short sword hard against his throat.

"Where did you get this sword?" demanded Vas-Sem.

"I found it" said Var trying to move his neck away from the sword edge.

"Where!" shouted Vas-Sem.

"Let me up and get this sword out of my face and I'll tell you" barked Var. Vas-Sem stood back still holding the sword out towards the tribesman. Var stood up and rubbed his throat.

"I was lost in the southern ocean and when I was out of options I had to surface. I came up next to one of your sea planes and the person on board opened fire on me. We fought and I killed him. The sword was lying on the deck."

"What did the man look like that you killed?" questioned the Dominator.

"He wore similar armour to you" stated Var as he remembered the dead man eyes. As he stared at the big warrior in front of him he saw the same glint in his eyes. Vas-Sem was struggling within; the sword he held pointed at Var was shaking with the effort of control. Part of him wanted to slice this upstart's throat, but his trained part restrained him and he lowered the blade.

"My father will decide on your fate" said Vas-Sem. He turned as if to leave but then spun quickly sending a lethal punch into Var's jaw. Vas-Sem bent down and hauled the unconscious tribesman over his shoulder.

The Lord Emperor was in the training room garbed in his baggy silk shorts and a silk jerkin. He was performing a complicated Kata. He stopped mid kick as Vas-Sem burst into the room. His son strode across the room and unceremoniously dropped the body he was carrying onto the matted floor. He then dropped to one knee and saluted.

"I am afraid I have grave news my lord" said Vas-Sem.

"Do you have news from the desert?" asked Lord Senn clearly confused and a little surprised as to why his son had dumped a body at his feet.

"No my Lord. It is concerning Bok" said Vas-Sem cautiously.

"What about him?" said the Emperor clearly disturbed.

"He had taken a sea blade out for a test run. I had been waiting for him to return so we could be on our way to the desert. When he didn't return I went looking for him. I found his craft and later found out this ocean man had killed him." Vas-Sem had purposely left out most of the story. His father looked down at the unconscious body. He was silent for a few moments and then responded.

"Does this mean you have not even started the desert mission?" asked Lord Senn. Vas-Sem was puzzled by the question, he had just given him news of his son's death and all he was worried about was a stupid mission.

"Yes my Lord, I thought..." the Emperor held up his hand to cut his son off mid sentence.

"I gave you a direct order" stated the Emperor still not looking at his son.

"You instructed me to retrieve Bok and then go to Ortha-Hab to find out what was happening" complained Vas-Sem. "I was simply following your orders."

"Do not try to twist my words. I know full well what I asked you to do. A man of your position could surely use his common sense and have gone without your brother" snarled the Emperor. Vas-Sem knew this was a futile argument. He had hoped the news of Bok's death would have somehow disinterested his father in everything else and given him some breathing space. He was mistaken and so quickly changed tact.

"I am sorry my Lord. I was concerned for my brother's safety; news of his loss has clouded my judgement. I am afraid there is more bad news to report." Vas-Sem's words were a great deal quieter.

"Go on" ordered his father.

"The Murai on Imercia have rebelled and have overthrown the fortress guard" reported Vas-Sem. His father had looked displeased before but with this news his lip curled and he clenched his fists in a clear attempt to control his temper. Vas-Sem knew if anyone else had delivered the news they could be missing a limb at this stage.

"The gate has been destroyed, there is no way back to Geb-Shu. I fought my way through and managed to drag this man through with me before the gate closed" continued Vas-Sem. The Emperor paced up and down the training room, lost in thought. He was interrupted by a groan from Var. He moved in close to his son and grasped him firmly by the shoulders.

"What of Ty and the squad, where are they now?" he asked.

"They await my return in Morlok-Tun my Lord" answered Vas-Sem.

"Good" said the Emperor. "Then go quickly and rejoin them and finish that mission, I must know what is happening in the Southern desert, and forgive me my earlier outburst, you are simply the bearer of tragic news. I will deal with this thing." He pointed towards Var.

"As you command father" said Vas-Sem reassured by his father's words. "What about Imercia? Do we still need the island? Surely we can be self sufficient here on Son-Gebshu?

"That maybe true my son, but that is not the issue. The Murai have set themselves against me. I must show them and show others that would follow suit what it means to stand against the Emperor. Now go, I will take care of this situation. You will join me on Imercia to celebrate my victory when you return."

"How will you get there if the gate is broken?" asked Vas-Sem.

"This is not the first time I have had to purge the surface of the planet, I have my ways" said the Emperor and he turned away. Vas-Sem knew his audience with his father was over.

*

Vas-Sem had been confused by his father's reaction. He was known for his unpredictability but the news of Bok's death didn't seem to register. Perhaps that was his way of dealing with emotion or perhaps his mother had been right. The Dominator pushed the absurd thoughts from his mind.

He strode from the gate chamber and spoke briefly with a guard. He continued out from the gatehouse and followed the directions he had been given. The big man walked through the dusty streets of Morlok-Tun and eventually arrived at the deserted barrack room. He searched the room already knowing that Ty-Sem would have left. He would have done the same thing if the situation had been reversed. He found nothing in the room so ventured on to the garage.

As he entered the garage the small replicator looked up from his work. He was grinding a component of some description in a vice cascading sparks, illuminating the scene. He stopped the grinder and lifted his goggles onto his forehead.

"How can I help you?" he said cheerfully.

"I am after news of the squad of Reavers who left on the last rotation." The replicator's demeanour immediately changed. He looked nervous and was trying desperately to avoid the Dominator's gaze.

"Umm, I'm not sure what you are talking about" stammered the man. Vas-Sem read the fat little man's body language with ease.

"Okay" said Vas-Sem calmly. "Let me tell you how this is going to go. You have two simple choices. One – you can tell me exactly what happened and I'll leave you as I found you or, two, you can pretend you don't know what I'm talking about and I will have to start grinding off parts of your body." The replicator was well aware this was no idle threat.

"Okay, Okay" he said quickly. "I'll tell you everything." He pushed the grinder farther away from the Dominator.

"They left in the remaining grounder in the afternoon of the last rotation. There was one big guy, a lot like yourself and five others. They all seemed to know what they were doing."

"Which way were they headed? And did they leave a mission route or any details?" asked Vas-Sem.

"Uh, yes they did." The replicator paused. "But I no longer have it," he said nervously.

"And why would that be?" asked Vas-Sem calmly.

"A man came in not long after they had left, he took the details and then left" replied the replicator.

"What man?" questioned the Dominator.

"I don't know who he was. I just assumed that was procedure, honestly" he pleaded. Vas-Sem reached across the work bench and picked up the grinder. He flicked the switch and the tool buzzed. The replicator flinched away from the tool.

"Okay, please don't hurt me. He was an administrator, maybe one of the Virtue's men."

"The Virtue of Water, Jinn-Aka?" asked Vas-Sem.

"Yes I think so" said the small man. Vas-Sem dropped the power tool onto the bench. "There is only one road to Ortha-Hab" added the replicator. "I had to put enough fuel in the grounder to get them there and back." Vas-Sem pondered the situation. There would be no reason to hide the mission unless Jinn-Aka himself was behind it and trying to keep whatever the secret was from his father. The mission notes could have proved useful, they would state the destination and the parameters and more than that would have been proof of them being here.

"Are there any vehicles left?" asked the Dominator.

"No they took the last working grounder; that one is just a shell" said the replicator pointing at the dusty vehicle. Vas-Sem leaned in closely to the small man.

"You must have something" he said as menacingly as he could manage. The small plump man sighed.

"There is my Argus, but it is my personal vehicle. It isn't part of the Emperor's vehicle fleet" complained the man.

"Everything is owned by the Emperor" said Vas-Sem and he cast a glance at the grinder on the bench.

"Okay" said the man in complete resignation. He went to the far end of the garage and removed a dust sheet. Beneath was a four wheeled buggy. It had a crude tubular roll cage encasing an engine and two seats. The wheels were exceptionally large and consisted of circular caterpillar tracks supported from the central hub by a series of suspension units. Vas-Sem had seen an Argus before but not with wheels like this.

"They are my special edition" said the replicator tapping the tracked wheel with his hand. "They will go over anything. Please be careful with her" he pleaded. Vas-Sem slid into the driver's seat and the vehicle suspension and the individual wheel suspension bounced to accommodate his weight. He started the engine and it purred as he revved the accelerator. The replicator opened the doors and Vas-Sem powered out.

The vehicle was a dream to drive; the suspension and unique traction of the wheels gave a smooth ride even over the roughest terrain. Vas-Sem poured on the power and slid the vehicle around a corner and out into the desert. He kept a sharp look out for anything unusual along the track. He stopped as he found some deep tracks veering off to the right. They were from a tracked vehicle that had been heading towards Morlok-Tun. Could be a grounder thought Vas-Sem. He remounted and continued on. He slowed as he came to a small bridge. He got out again and looked at the bridge. It was an anomaly. Although it was constructed of worn timber all of the fixings were brand new and stood out in stark contrast against the older materials. He looked out into the gorge below and it dawned on him what had happened. Re-seated in the Argus he back tracked and followed the tread prints of the grounder in the baked dirt. As he descended down he could make out something in the distance. He slowed his speed as the blackened husk of the grounder came into view. He stopped a short distance away. Before checking the burnt out vehicle he ran up the embankment to the left. He saw more caterpillar tracks from a second vehicle and numerous boot prints. As he walked along the ridge he saw several silver cans. He picked one up. It was a brand of liquor. Whoever had been here had waited some time.

He ran back down the bank across to the vehicle. The rear door was shut. He tried the catch but the heat of the fire had welded it shut. He removed his war hammer and smashed it against the handle. He jumped back as the heavy door thumped into the dust.

A charred skeleton rolled down the ramp. Vas-Sem peered inside the rear compartment and saw the other remains inside.

"I'm sorry Ty" he said.

He walked around the grisly scene noticing the hundreds of gun spikes lying in the dust and the shattered caterpillar track. It was a planned ambush but how would they have known that Bok and I were not inside he thought.

*

Var dragged himself up to a sitting position, his jaw aching as did his head. He stared at the man in front of him. He practised a pattern of moves with exquisite finesse. The flow of movements was seamless and the power controlled. Whoever this is thought Var he is a master. The Lord Emperor stopped his practise and turned to look at his newly awakened guest.

"I am glad you could join me" said Lord Senn. Var stared at him blankly.

"Please come and help me practise" and the Emperor gestured to a position on the mat in front of him. Var knew how this would go. He stood and took his place opposite the Emperor. The Emperor bowed slightly and then stood back in a practised stance with the majority of his weight on his back foot. Var simply stood still his hands at his side. The Emperor twisted his front foot and then thrust his rear leg out towards Var's face. Var stepped back and the foot stopped just short of its target. Lord Senn held his foot in place for a moment longer than needed and then snapped it back.

He jumped forward again kicking with the same leg and aiming for Var's ribcage in a roundhouse motion. Var instinctively brought his arm up to protect himself. At the last moment the Emperor changed target and his instep slapped against Var's face. As Var absorbed the blow the Emperor followed it up with a hammer fist to the same spot. The force knocked the tribesman to his knees. Lord Senn stepped away.

Var felt the inside of his mouth with his tongue and could taste the blood. He stood and smiled revealing a bloody grin. Lord Senn attacked again this time using his front foot to kick out. Var read the move and caught the front foot. He then went to kick out the Emperor's supporting leg. The Emperor using his held foot as a pivot jumped, swinging his supporting foot around thundering his heel into Var's already sore jaw. Var was knocked from his feet by the blow and landed in a heap.

He picked himself up and spat out a piece of tooth onto the pristine mats. He circled his jaw trying to ease the pain. The Emperor jumped again this time spinning in the air and outstretching his arm in an attempt to backfist his opponent. Var blocked the strike but the Emperor reversed his body weight sending an elbow into Var's ribcage. He turned about to strike down across Var's clavicle. Var fought the pain in his side and punched upwards. His knuckles clouted the Emperor square in the chin. Lord Senn smiled. He lifted his front leg and hammered it down onto Var's shoulder before twisting his hips and firing his leg out whilst looking over his shoulder. The power of the kick launched Var into the air and he landed with a thud, his breath escaping.

The Emperor loomed over the winded man. He was tossing a short sword from blade to hilt over and over in his hand.

"So ocean man, you killed my son?" said Lord Senn. Var rolled his eyes, my luck must change soon he thought.

"I didn't know he was your son" said Var.

"How did he die?" asked the Emperor.

"I drowned him" snarled Var blood trickling from the corner of his mouth.

"Are you sure he was dead?" asked the Emperor. Var frowned at the question.

"He has gone to the depths. I watched as his breath gave out." Var was attempting to goad the man, without success.

"Well my ocean friend it seems as if I owe you a debt of gratitude" said Lord Senn. Var had no idea what the madman was talking about.

"For your service to me and for being such a good martial opponent I shall return the favour. As you are a man of the ocean, we will let your own gods determine your guilt. You will undergo the trial of the ocean."

Var shrugged, surely he had seen everything the ocean could throw at him. How bad could it be?

*

As Vas-Sem drove the Argus away the fading light picked out the freshly dug graves on the hillside. His destination was the outlying town of Ortha-Hab. He pulled the vehicle in close to a small hill overlooking the town; the tracked wheels moulding over the rough terrain and shuddering as the engine died.

The small town of Ortha-Hab consisted of dozens of low domed circular buildings all huddled close to the foothills. They seemed afraid to stretch out into the vast expanse of desert plain ahead. A much larger structure lay a short distance from the town. Whatever it had been the sands and winds had eroded the walls and softened its lines so it was now a mere ghost of its former grandeur. A few more revolutions and the ancient ruin would become part of the natural landscape.

Vas-Sem studied the view for some time. There were plenty of tracks criss-crossing the main route into the town, and in amongst the buildings there were a few old desert vehicles, but no sign of a grounder. He unpacked his desert cloak from his kit bag and threw it around his shoulders. The dark brown cloak covered him completely concealing his ceramic armour. It was threadbare were it dragged on the ground. He flicked the large hood over his head and started down the hill towards the town, the last remnants of light casting a long shadow out behind him.

He made his way quietly through the deserted streets. Apart from the soft orange glow coming from the tiny window slits, there were very few signs of life. From his hillside vantage point he had tried to gauge which dwelling could have passed for that of the Missionrai in charge, but nothing stood out. All the buildings were built from the same materials and the same design, only additional extensions and alterations told them apart. He heard laughter and immediately headed in that direction. He saw the two clasped hands symbol branded into a sign hanging outside the door. The symbol was an ancient one which indicated a place of meeting. The original meaning had long been lost and it now symbolised a drinking establishment. The best place to find a Reaver squad in this place thought Vas-Sem.

As he entered the tavern the laughter and chatter ceased as if someone had quickly turned the volume down. The assembled eyes watched as the giant cloaked figure strode towards the bar. Without removing his hood Vas-Sem carefully gauged the clientele. There were two elderly men on his left playing a game of chattal, the clear chink of the stone counters could be heard on the slate gaming board. To his right was a single man nursing a stone flagon. Judging by his demeanour it looked like he had been nursing it for some time. Close to the bar were four men seated in high backed settles. They wore armour but not complete sets as some pieces were too big or small and from different armour patterns.

The barman was old, his features weathered by the winds like the ruin that lay outside. He gave the big man a false smile revealing his lack of teeth.

"Grotch" stated Vas-Sem. The bartender nodded and proceeded to pour a sweet smelling liquid into a handled stone drinking vessel. The four men continued their conversation now ignoring the newcomer.

"You are a stranger here on the desert's edge fellow. What is your business here in Ortha?" asked the barman.

"I am on the Emperor's business" answered Vas-Sem in a loud, steady voice. The four men stopped talking and stared again at the stranger. This time Vas-Sem stared back. The nearest man went to rise but he was knocked back into his seat as the Dominator smashed the stone tankard into his face, the vessel shattered and stone shards buried themselves into the man's face and neck.

With one deft movement Vas-Sem unsheathed his belt knife and rammed it into the open mouth of the man sat opposite. The knife came out the back of his head and pinned him to the wooden seat. The two remaining Reavers now trapped behind their dead friends scrambled to get their nail guns free and primed.

A fierce clack echoed as Vas-Sem's war hammer smashed into the hand of the one Reaver who had managed to get his weapon clear. The blow shattered the bones in his hand and he dropped the gun onto the table, screaming as he withdrew his battered hand. The scream ended abruptly as the war hammer tore a hole in his skull. His eyes rolled and he slumped forward onto the table, spilling the precious liquid over the table. Vas-Sem hauled the first man out of his seat and onto the floor. He sat down and slid in next to the dead body, his eyes firmly fixed on the remaining survivor.

"Gun" ordered Vas-Sem. He held out his hand. The frightened man obeyed and slid his gun across the table. The big man picked up the weapon pulled back the slide and flicked the switch. At the same time he pressed the release catch and the magazine dropped clear. He pulled the trigger and the chambered round thunked into the seat opposite and he tossed the gun aside.

"Who ordered the ambush on the grounder?" he asked.

"What grounder?" stammered the man. Vas-Sem reached across and grabbed hold of one of the Reaver's fingers. He bent it upwards sharply, snapping it cleanly. The man yelled and looked in disbelief at his distorted digit.

"Would you like me to ask you again?" said Vas-Sem.

"No" replied the man. "A man came. He was from the city; a servant of the Virtue I think. It was him that ordered us to prepare an ambush".

"What else?" asked Vas-Sem.

"He told us a grounder would be coming out this way. We were to stop it ever reaching Ortha and kill all on board" replied the nervous Reaver.

"Did the servant give the reasons behind the attack?" questioned Vas-Sem.

"Why would he?" said the man. "We are soldiers; we just followed the orders. The only action we ever get is shooting desert vraks; nothing much else happens out here. We were glad of the action, that and the fact he gave us a grounder of our own full of weapons and ammo. Our squad leader told us that they were traitors to the Emperor." Vas-Sem stared hard at the frightened man.

"Where is your squad leader now?" demanded the Dominator.

"He has gone to the city to report back to the Virtue. He didn't want to go but we insisted. This is what this is all about isn't it?" he paused. "The mistake."

"What mistake would that be?" asked Vas-Sem.

"That there were only six bodies instead of eight." Vas-Sem sat in silence contemplating the man's words. Jinn-Aka was behind this, but his reason Vas-Sem could not fathom. If it was a move against the Emperor, then why kill his sons and not the Emperor himself. Perhaps it was to drag the Emperor out here. Whatever the reasons, the Virtue of Water held the answers and would be his next stop.

"What is your squad leader's name?" asked Vas-Sem as he stood up.

"Clo-Te" answered the man. "Are you going to kill me now?" he asked. Vas-Sem threw his hood back over his head.

"The men you butchered were all faithful soldiers of the Emperor, including a fellow Dominator. It is the Virtue that has played you false. If you have any honour as a soldier of the Emperor you'll know what is due. I'll leave you to decide your own fate."

As the dark cloaked figure left the tavern he heard the whirr and click of a nail gun as the remaining Reaver passed judgement on himself.

*

Lord Senn was in an unusually buoyant mood. The preparations were going well for the forthcoming planetfall that, coupled with the news that the Virtue of Water had arrived, meant all of his plans were coming together. He was secretly glad of the Murai revolt as it had been many revolutions since he had felt so invigorated. The thought of battle however quick it would be had made him eager to re-establish his hold on the worlds he controlled.

He was seated at his desk in his ante-chamber where he conducted most state business. The room was lavishly decorated with plush drapes and the oldest and most exquisite furniture and antiquities filled every space. Along one wall hung a series of portraits showing the great Emperors of history. There was a knock at the door and Cho-Sem, one of his Dominators entered.

"Lord, The Virtue of Water is here to see you" he said.

"Very Good Cho. Send him in" replied Lord Senn. The striking figure of Jinn-Aka entered, a broad smile on his face. The two men embraced formally and then clasped hands in genuine friendship.

"Have a seat my friend" said Lord Senn as he gestured towards a chair. Both men sat.

"So…., good news I hope?" enquired the Emperor.

"Indeed my Lord. My man has just recently returned with the news. It has taken longer than we expected but the result is what you wanted" stated the Virtue.

"I admit I had expected you sooner, but my eldest had delayed his departure due to some misunderstanding. I sent him out directly. I hope there weren't any problems?" asked the Emperor.

"No my Lord. It went exactly as planned. All were burnt to a crisp inside the vehicle." replied the Virtue hiding his nervousness.

"Excellent my friend. What about the men you used. I hope there are no loose ends there?" questioned Lord Senn.

"None my Lord, I have been thorough in covering..." he paused, "The loose ends."

The Lord Emperor rose and walked towards an ornately decorated cupboard. He carefully removed two silver chalices and a decanter.

"There is news you are headed to the planet to quell an uprising?" Jinn-Aka asked.

"That's correct" smiled the Emperor as he poured out the blood red liquid. "The nameless have decided to test my resolve so I am preparing for a little adventure." He winked at the Virtue and handed him a drink. The

Emperor sat back on the desk and swigged the liquid. He wiped his mouth and sat back in his chair. Jinn-Aka studied the Emperor watching for any sign. There was nothing, so he reclined and drank the smooth liquid. The Virtue lent forward to place the empty chalice on the desk. As he did, his vision swam and he misjudged the distance, the cup clanking onto the floor. His hands went to his throat as he felt it constrict. The Emperor stood over the dying man.

"You thought to hide details from me" he yelled. "Or did you forget to tell me the body count was one short." Jinn-Aka looked confused. He had been keeping the detail from the Emperor but it was the fact the body count was two men short." He knew then what the Emperor did not and smiled as blood trickled from the corner of his mouth.

"Loo-se en-ds" chuckled the Virtue.

"Exactly" replied the Emperor.

*

Var awoke early; the cold stone floor had not provided for a comfortable nights rest. His body ached and his newly acquired bruises adorned his body like medals of achievement. Even with his optimistic outlook on the world he felt alone and lost. It was not self pity but the fact he had failed to keep his promise to Bronsur and his family. Var started at the sound of keys and a Reaver appeared in the doorway.

"On your feet fish boy" ordered the guard. He was led from the cell and briskly marched through the corridors. They entered the familiar gate room and Var recognised the sparking pillars of the Lexan gate. The gateway was already open and the magical aura in the centre bent the light as it pulsed. The guard shoved Var towards the gate; he stared sideways at the chanting servillisor before he disappeared into the void.

As he rolled clear at the other end of the portal he raised his arms to shield his eyes from the great light of Shu. He had emerged from an identical portal although unlike the other he had travelled through, this one stood open to the elements. It was perched on top of a small island which was surrounded on all sides by endless ocean. As Var's eyes adjusted to the bright light he could see the winding track from the gate led to a huge stone tower which stood guard over a formidable walled harbour. The outpost was full of movement; armoured men were busy carrying and lifting supplies to the anchored fleet of sea blades.

His guard gave him a shove and then followed him closely down to the staging point. As he drew nearer he could make out the imposing figure that he had sparred against. He was gesturing and commanding the men surrounding him. He noticed the prisoner.

"Ah my young sparring partner" he said quite jovially. "Cho, put him aboard my barge. We have some unfinished business." Var was bundled aboard the Emperor's launch. The boat was different to the sea planes Var had seen before; it was a huge hulk of metal that tapered to a point at the bow. It didn't have the wings like the sea blades. Instead it had four massive fans in the flattened stern and two arms at the front that extended down into the ocean. Var was led onto the barge at the rear and he looked down through the metal grill and the fan blades that were slowly spinning beneath. Cho-Sem led him to one side and gestured towards the floor. Var sat.

He watched as the Emperor and his retinue boarded the craft. Moments later the gigantic fans hummed into life and the vessel lurched forward. As the great ship cleared the harbour walls the pitch of the fans increased and Var felt the ship tilt backwards, the rear deck now only a short distance from the ocean surface. The barge was now in full flight; the two front arms held a 'V' shaped fin on which the massive craft now aquaplaned.

They continued for some time until Var noticed the pitch change again. This time the craft slowed. The engine subsided still further until it now just ticked over, with the blades making a loud 'dub-dub' sound. Two of the Emperor's retinue walked across the rear deck and started to throw bits of fish, blood and what looked like entrails into the sea. The vessel slowly turned leaving the red detritus in a large circle.

"Man the guns" commanded the Emperor. "Only shoot anything trying to board the ship. Helmsman ready on the throttle."

The Emperor walked towards the rear of the vessel and gestured to Cho-Sem to bring the prisoner. Var could see the huge ship now floated in the centre of red halo; he could also see the black shapes darting beneath the waves. With horror he realised what Lord Senn had in store for him and he tried to stop his advance towards the edge. The Emperor turned to face his prisoner.

"You admitted to killing my son without provocation. According to our laws your life is now forfeit. As devastated as I am by my loss, I have decided to show you compassion. As a man of the sea, we will return you to it and let the great oceans of Gebshu decide your fate."

Var gritted his teeth and was about to shout back at his tormentor when he felt a hard push in the back and he vaulted headlong over the end of the ship and into the sea. As the bubbles cleared he could see hundreds of black figures swimming at speed around him. As he tried to comprehend the situation a blurred figure of a kekken came sharply into focus, its fanged maw gaping. Var closed his eyes and prayed to Povian.

Chapter 8 – Storm

Vas-Sem drove through the night to reach Morlok-Tun by first light. The Replicator had been very grateful and very surprised by the return of his beloved Argus. In his gratitude he had told Vas-Sem that the city guards had been instructed to arrest and detain the Dominator as a traitor to the Emperor. Vas-Sem weighed his options. Return to his father and expose the Virtue of Water or confront Jinn-Aka to discover his real motives. He decided on the latter.

Still dressed in his desert garb the big man crept silently along the alleyway. He crouched down at the end of the narrow passage and looked out across the busy street towards the Municipal building. The grand structure overwhelmed everything around it. It had six large pillars on top of a stepped plinth which supported the overhanging roof. Its square shape was topped by a pyramid equal in height to that of the lofty pillars. There were two Reavers on guard and plenty more milling in and out. The building was the administration centre for the District of Water which stretched from Mount Timoris out beyond the Ortha-Hab desert to Mount Illera in the far North.

Vas-Sem surveyed the building. Trying to gain access without bloodshed would be impossible and certain suicide. An idea flashed into his mind and he stood and bounded back to the Replicator's garage. The small man was busy cleaning and polishing his recently returned desert buggy. He looked up at the big Dominator and sighed heavily.

"You want to borrow it again don't you?" he asked. Vas-Sem smiled.

"No, that's not why I am here, but I do need your help again." He turned and looked at the derelict grounder in the adjacent bay. "Does the mounted gun on that thing still work?" he asked.

"I think it does" answered the puzzled Replicator.

"Well" said Vas-Sem. "Help me free it from the grounder and get it working."

"I'm not sure I should be helping a traitor" he replied nervously. Vas-Sem swivelled and stared at the grubby little man.

"You help me get this free and then you can go to the authorities and tell them where I am. I am sure they will be grateful for the information." The Replicator stood and walked past the big man.

"I was going to report you anyway" he said. "But as you didn't resort to more threats of violence, I'll help you."

"That was my next plan" said Vas-Sem trying to hide a slight smirk.

The two men worked together in silence to remove the heavy weapon from the vehicle. Even with Vas-Sem's considerable strength it was a struggle to lift. The Replicator expertly slid the cartridges in and out and checked the firing mechanism; he removed the circular magazine clip and banged it on the workbench.

"Empty" he muttered. He moved to the back of the workshop and moved several boxes which made him cough as the dust swirled around his nose. He stood up proudly clutching another magazine in his hands.

"Knew I had one somewhere" he said to himself. He slotted the magazine home and placed his hands on his hips to admire his work. Vas-Sem flicked the compressor switch but nothing happened. He stared accusingly at the Replicator.

"It won't work without power" he said as if talking to a child. "It normally runs off the power cells in the grounder" he added as he saw the anger on the Dominators face.

"Can we not use one of them?" asked Vas-Sem. The Replicator was about to make another sarcastic comment but stopped himself.

"Not really. They weigh almost the same as the gun. We could use a portable cell from one of my power tools but it would drain fairly quickly."

"Would it be enough to deploy a magazine?" asked Vas-Sem.

"Maybe" said the Replicator as he shrugged his shoulders.

"It will have to do" said Vas-Sem. The small man attached the portable power cell under the rear loading chamber and connected it to the gun's compressor. He flicked the switch and the compressor hummed as the air chamber filled. The Replicator flicked the switch again to kill the power.

"Well it works, but I have no idea for how long."

"It will be long enough" said Vas-Sem. "Perhaps you would give me a few moments to make my escape before you report me?" The Replicator looked surprised by the question.

"I wasn't really going to report you" he answered.

"I think you should" stated Vas-Sem. "If they found out you had helped me and didn't report it you'd be in serious trouble."

"Good point. If you don't mind me saying you don't strike me as the traitorous type" he suggested.

"I think only time will determine that" said the Dominator. He turned to face the Replicator. "One more thing, what is your name?"

"Ton-l, my name is Ton-l" replied the surprised man. No soldier of the Emperor had ever asked his name before.

"Thank you Ton-l" said Vas-Sem. He hoisted the gun from the floor and heaved it onto his shoulder. Ton-l watched in awe as the big Dominator left the garage seemingly unaffected by his heavy load.

After several false starts Ton-l made his way into the street and towards the great town building. As he mounted the stone steps one of the Reavers moved to intercept him.

"What business do you have here?" he demanded.

"I have news of the traitor" said Ton-l. The Reaver looked at him suspiciously.

"Follow me" he said curtly. Ton-l followed the guard through the great doors into the cavernous entrance hall. The Reaver reported to a seated Missionrai who beckoned the Replicator over. Ton-l regaled his story to the very serious soldier.

"How long ago?" he barked.

"Only a few moments, that's all" replied Ton-l wishing he had not bothered. The Missionrai shouted orders which echoed throughout the great hall. Dozens of soldiers appeared all checking weapons and gun clips. The Missionrai turned to Ton-l.

"Show us" he commanded.

Ton-I filed out of the building and down the steps, the swarm of soldiers following closely. They entered the street and the busy town's people quickly parted to let them through.

Vas-Sem watched Ton-I lead the Reavers from the building and waited for the right moment. He lifted the heavy gun upright and rested the multiple barrels on the low wall in front of him. He was situated on the roof of a single storey building opposite the Municipal. He flicked the switch and the compressor started to hum. He grabbed the handles and squeezed the trigger. The powerful weapon opened up on the unaware soldiers ripping through armour and flesh. Caught in the confusion they didn't know whether to run or dive for cover. In their hesitation the metal shards ended all indecision. Vas-Sem kept his finger firmly pressed on the trigger trying to make every salvo count. The compressor moaned and then quickly died as the power cells gave up the last of their energy.

In the panic Ton-I had dived into the dusty road and covered his head with his hands. As silence drifted across the massacre he rolled onto his back and sat up. He baulked at the sight of the fallen soldiers. Heavy spikes protruded from their bodies and blood had started to stain the ground. The Missionrai who had been behind him coughed and spat blood onto the floor. Two bolts were buried deep in his back. He glared at the frightened man.

"You led us into this trap, you nameless dog" cursed the Missionrai. He drew a short sword and moved forwards. Ton-I who was desperately trying to scurry backwards raised his arms across his eyes, not wanting to see the final blow. The blow never came. He dropped his arm to see the dark outline of Vas-Sem withdrawing his knife from the man's neck and lowering the body to the ground. The Dominator nodded and turned away. He leapt up the steps and disappeared inside the Municipal.

As he entered the vast hallway he drew both of his war hammers. He banged the end of one on a domed metal boss on his opposite forearm. The hit activated a mechanism and segments of metal unfolded to form a small circular buckler. He repeated the action on his other arm.

Almost all of the guards had emptied out after the Replicator, only two remained blocking the path of the Dominator. The two men couldn't have been more opposite. One was tall and thin with a determined grimace on his face. The other was short and plump and looked like he would rather be anywhere else.

"Nameless traitor!" spat the taller man.

Vas-Sem ignored the insult and walked towards the two men. As he did he removed a metal disc from his belt. The circular ring had a sharp edge around its circumference and was dissected by a thin bar which Vas-Sem's fingers were now wrapped around. In a single movement he dropped to one knee and flung his arm in a wide arc releasing the disc. The first man was in the process of drawing his gun and lurched to one side. The disc missed him by a slither. The second man had remained bolted to the spot and the disc thunked into his shoulder plate ricocheting across the room, burying itself in the wall. The small man, still unmoving, looked down cautiously at the long dent in his armour.

The tall man opened fire with his gun but Vas-Sem was too close. Several shards bounced off his armour and bucklers before his hammer smashed into the gun splintering it across the mirrored floor. As the tall man tried to recover and draw his mace, the Dominator's second hammer thudded into the side of his kneecap shattering the bone. The man buckled as his leg gave way. Before he reached the floor the armoured knee of Vas-Sem rammed into his face, cracking teeth and bone.

The Dominator stepped over the mangled body and gave a sideways glance as he passed the small man who still hadn't moved. He climbed the regal staircase and stood facing the open double doors of the Virtue's office. Sat behind the Virtue's desk was the Servitor Tol-ith. The Servitor sect were the brightest of all the Dumonii and provided the organisation and management behind the military administration. Although confined to a desk most Servitors were accomplished in martial skills, often choosing to study ancient methods of combat rather than the crude strength based styles used by most. Tol-ith had been Jinn-Aka's Servitor for more than fourteen revolutions. He was as loyal to the Virtue as were any of the Emperor's retinue.

He wore a dark blue tunic which was held in place by a wide leather belt. He had short black hair and a distinctive angular face. His open tunic revealed the tattoos of his sect, ancient text taken from the vast library of the Servitors. He was sitting with hands folded staring unblinking at the intruder that stood in the doorway.

"Welcome Vas-Sem; please come in" said Tol-ith. The Dominator walked in without hesitation. As he passed the doors the two guards secreted behind them flung them shut and levelled active guns at Vas-Sem's back.

"It seems you were expecting me" said Vas-Sem cordially. "Is your master here, or is he in hiding?" The remark touched a nerve with the loyal Servitor but he quelled his anger.

"He is with your father I believe and now you have arrived I will be able to clear up at least one of his loose ends" said Tol-ith.

"Like you did out in the desert" growled Vas-Sem.

"They were unfortunate losses and as it turns out unnecessary as neither you or your brother were inside" mused Tol-ith.

"You and your Virtue of Filth will never get away with this. When my father finds out you'll be...."

"What do you mean?" interrupted Tol-ith. "When he finds out? The honourable Virtue of Water was simply following your father's orders."

"Liar!" yelled Vas-Sem. He swung his left arm backward with such speed and force he knocked the Reaver clean off his feet slamming him into the wall. The other Reaver squeezed the trigger and the metal rounds pinged off the Dominator's armour. Vas-Sem swung his other arm back smashing the buckler into the man's face but not before several spikes had penetrated the joints in his armour.

As the man staggered back holding his bloody face, Vas-Sem reversed his war hammer and swung it hard at the injured guard. The hammer spike neatly penetrated the Reaver's chest plate, puncturing his heart. Vas-Sem winced as the first guard had crawled along the floor and lunged with his knife stabbing the Dominator in the back of his calf. He quickly withdrew the hammer from the dead man's chest and thundered the hammer into his attacker's skull. The massive blow punched a square hole through the guard's helmet, the hammerhead forcing the metal and bone fragments into his brain.

Vas-Sem reached down and removed the blade from his leg. He tried to reach around to his shoulder but he could not reach the offending spikes. The pain flared in his shoulder and he felt his warm blood slowly seep into his under shirt. He grimaced and turned to face the still seated Servitor. Tol-ith stood and took the ornate sword that was displayed on the desk and drew the slightly curved blade.

He leapt from the floor onto the table and in one elegant move span in the air as he brought the glinting blade down towards Vas-Sem. The Dominator brought up his buckler to block the sword blow. The ornate blade clattered against the small shield boss breaking several segments. He landed and whirled the blade in his hand before thrusting it towards Vas-Sem's stomach. The Dominator brought his hammer across his body to deflect the blow as he took one step backward to steady himself. Tol-ith was a master swordsman and Vas-Sem slowed by his injuries was in trouble.

He fought off blow after blow, his hammer shafts and his forearms taking the brunt of the continuous damage. The big man was starting to breathe hard and the pooled sweat was starting to sting his eyes. He had to do something and soon. He feigned an attack with his left hammer purposely dropping his guard with his right. Tol-ith immediately saw the opening and thrust at the Dominator's open side. The razor sharp blade slid past his abdominal plate and into his side above the hip. The Dominator did not try and avoid the strike instead stepping in slightly to meet the blow. Tol-ith realised the plan as one of Vas-Sem's massive gauntleted hands clamped down around the Servitor's hand and the other fist slammed into his jaw. Tol-ith was launched across the room by the force of the blow, cracking his head on the Virtues' desk as he landed. His head swam and he watched the big man draw the sword from his body and snap it under foot.

Vas-Sem picked up the dazed Servitor by his jerkin and hoisting him to his feet. He slammed another right hook into his ribcage doubling him over. He then brought his knee up into his face, throwing the helpless Servitor back violently. Vas-Sem drew his knife and the blood stained Dominator knelt beside the flattened Servitor. He placed the tip of the knife at Tol-ith's eye. Tol-ith coughed and blood oozed from the cuts in his ruined mouth.

"I may be many things but I am no liar." The words were difficult for the Servitor to form.

"Do you expect me to believe that my father ordered my death?" demanded Vas-Sem.

"I know how it must look" said Tol-ith. "But neither I nor the Virtue would do anything without the Emperor's approval. You must know that is the truth. I have no idea of your father's motives. He is the Emperor and his word is law." Vas-Sem withdrew his knife and sheathed it. He sat back exhausted, his adrenaline subsiding and the pain starting to overwhelm him.

"My mother was right after all" he sighed.

"What do you mean?" asked Tol-ith as he too attempted to sit.

"She told me that my father believes he is the Emperor of the prophecy and that one day my brother or I would turn on him and kill him. She said a madness had overtaken him and his paranoia stretched to all those loyal to him. I believed it was her way of vengeance against my father."

At that moment the door burst open and a thin man flanked by a surly Reaver entered the room. The breathless man stared hard trying to understand the scene before him.

"Servitor! Are you alright?" he shouted.

"I will live, at least for the moment" coughed Tol-ith.

"I have grave news. I have just returned from the great city."

"Where is the Virtue?" asked Tol-ith.

"That is the news. I am sorry to report that he is dead."

"What!?" spluttered the shocked Servitor.

"It seems I am not the only one affected by the madness" added Vas-Sem. Tol-ith looked at the Dominator and then back at the ashen faced messenger.

"How did he die?" asked Tol-ith.

"It's not clear. The official statement from the palace was that his heart gave out. The Emperor ordered a quick private burial due to the fact he was embarking on an ocean world campaign" replied the messenger.

"I think we all know that is a lie" spat Tol-ith. He turned to Vas-Sem.

"It looks like we have all been overtaken by the Emperor's madness. The district of water and the remains of its forces are yours to command, as am I if you will allow it" said Tol-ith. The Dominator hauled himself to his feet clearly in considerable pain.

"What is your command?" asked Tol-ith.

"I could do with a Medicator" said Vas-Sem as he tried to stifle a smile.

*

Var kicked hard to the left trying to avoid the gaping maw of the oncoming creature. The Kekken closed quickly but instead of attacking it veered away sharply. Var could hear the dull clicking noises coming from the throng and guessed that they were communicating. He looked to the surface and could see the shimmering black hulls of the craft above. He would have a better chance up there he thought and was about to kick up when taloned fingers firmly grasped his arms.

The two Kekkens holding him flicked their tails in unison and Var found himself descending rapidly into the depths. His breath was holding but his lungs were starting to burn. From out of the darkness swam another Kekken. It was clearly much larger than the others. It was carrying something which was streaming bubbles out behind it. The creature halted in front of Var and held out the object. Var looked in astonishment at the antique breather unit clutched in the animal's claws. The two other creatures released their grip and Var gratefully grabbed the unit and bit down on the mouthpiece breathing in the precious oxygen.

The Kekken in front of him moved his hand across his chest and made the symbol;

    < Friend >

Var hadn't imagined it. He was sure that his previous encounter with the creature had been nothing more than a consequence of movements. This latest encounter clearly showed it was purposeful which meant intelligence. The creature slowly reached out towards Var and his long talon gently traced the scar on Var's face. He grabbed Var's arms suddenly around the wrist on each arm. It dug what resembled a thumb into his forearm as if attempting to take his pulse.

Suddenly Var jerked with pain. An intense pressure flared in his mind. He shook his head violently trying to shake free the torment. The Kekken's grip held fast and the flood of agony continued. He opened his eyes and stared directly into the dark glassy orbs of the creature. As he stared ahead the pain eased and he could hear a whispering voice.

[Do not fight] [Do not fight]

The voice repeated the mantra. Var was struggling to comprehend the situation. The creature he had thought a mindless sea monster had given him air and was now attempting to communicate with thought. He calmed himself and tried to let himself fall into the situation. As he did the pain subsided. A thousand questions ricocheted inside his mind.

[Focus]

Var could clearly understand the command coming from the Kekken. He tried to comply.

[Better]

Var formed the question in his mind and held it there.

[Why?]

[We are one, our lives are now joined] came the response. Thoughts entered Var's mind uninvited.

[We are not monsters. There is much we can learn from each other. You are safe among us]

Var looked past the Kekken to which he was bonded to the hordes of animals that swam close by all staring with interest at the ocean man. Var tried again to focus his mind on a question.

[What do you want from me?]

[We are the custodians of the ocean. We want nothing from you. You saved us from death. We will repay our debt to you]

Var's thoughts jumped again.

[What about the men above?]

[They are a blind and ignorant race. They think they bait us with blood. They think they hunt us. They have long since forgotten who we once were. Our numbers are vast. It is we who hunt them.]

[They intend to attack my friends on an island called Imercia] thought Var.

[They will not make it. A great storm approaches. The ocean surface will erupt and destroy them. We will take you to the island]

A nearby Kekken swam in and placed a small black charm on a necklace around his neck.

[Use this when you would speak with us again]

Before Var could form another thought the Kekken released his thumbs and broke the connection. Var felt light headed as the shock of the telepathic link faded. He held the strange charm in his hand. It was a piece of coral carved into a totem, the bottom half portraying a man and the top half a Kekken. A small hole had been drilled through it and moving in the middle was a small crystal orb. As he studied the piece the two Kekkens grabbed his arms again and started to propel him through the ocean.

The speed was exhilarating. Even though they carried their less than streamline passenger the creatures moved at incredible speed through the water. Var felt hugely privileged traversing the ocean amongst these intelligent and noble creatures. He marvelled at their grace and power of movement and thought how ignorant his own race was in comparison. He realised in that moment that they were born into this environment and completely at one with it, whereas the ocean peoples, although they lived in harmony with their surroundings, were born to breathe air and walk on the land above the ocean.

*

In the moons that had passed since the Murai had taken the Imercian fortress, Muyda had been busy rebuilding and preparing. She had been grateful for the help the two giants had given but felt a pang of guilt that she had not told them what would happen to their friend back on Son-Gebshu.

She had organised living quarters for all of the surviving Murai inside the fortress. It now crawled with people working under her guidance. They had removed the heavy guns from the sea-blade fleet and mounted them at intervals around the outer wall. The mouth to the harbour had been blocked by scuttled vessels and the Lexan gate had been completely destroyed. The corpses of the Dumonii guards had been piled and burnt; the dead townspeople had been reverently placed in a mass stone tomb at the other end of the island. The few ocean tribes that had been part of the Murai had asked for their fallen comrades to be returned to the ocean. In her last act of cleansing Muyda had instructed the demolition of the driftwood town. She had envisaged a new curtain wall extending from the fortress that would have enveloped the old shanty town. This would become a communal area for craft and trade. She was confident that she could rebuild a functioning civilisation on the island, although the threat of retaliation from the Emperor permanently plagued her thoughts. She knew he wouldn't be able to let their actions go unanswered.

Gero had constructed a huge wooden A frame from the salvaged township timber. With the aid of several Murai and a sturdy pulley block he was hoisting a large load of building stone to the top of the newly constructed wall. Muyda approached the giant.

"Is there anything else you need Gero?" she asked. Gero tossed his head in the direction of his father who was sat on a barrel watching his son's efforts.

"You can give that old goat something to do instead of sitting there advising me" he smiled. Muyda smiled back at the giant and placed her hand on his massive forearm.

"I really am grateful to you and your father for staying to help us. It has given everyone a sense of hope and a sense of safety."

"Please" said Gero holding up his hands. He was about to continue when he stared out over Muyda's head.

"We have a visitor" said the giant nodding towards the beach. Muyda swung to see a long haired young man striding through the shallows and onto the beach. He gathered his hair behind his head and squeezed out the water.

"Told you he'd be back" said Hanelore.

"Is that your friend?" asked a shocked Muyda.

"It is" said Gero. "He seems to have the knack of survival."

Var approached the strange trio.

"Don't I even get a hug?" said Var holding out his arms to the giant. Gero gave him a manly slap on the shoulder.

"Good to see you little Var" said Gero.

"He thought you were dead" said Hanelore pointing at his son.

"Good to see you too Hanelore" chuckled Var.

"This is Muyda" said Gero introducing her.

"I am honoured to meet you." Muyda grabbed his hands in hers. "I am deeply sorry for what happened to you. I know what you must have been through." She stroked the obvious contusion on his arm. "I have no idea how you managed to escape but you are truly welcome here."

"To be honest" started Var, "I am still a little unsure what happened myself. Although I do know that a huge storm is heading this way. You should probably start lashing things down and get people inside."

"You are a fortune teller now?" asked Gero.

"Something like that" replied Var with a wink.

Var had enjoyed reliving his story and watching the expressions on the giants' faces as he told them of his adventure. Muyda had remained quite sombre, the news from Son-Gebshu and the Emperor had brought back painful memories.

"I don't believe you" scoffed Hanelore. "Intelligent fish, I've never heard such rubbish."

"We don't know everything father" scolded Gero.

"You may not boy, but I have seen all there is to see of this watery world" replied Hanelore.

"You'll see for yourself when I leave" said Var defiantly.

"You're leaving?" asked a surprised Muyda.

"I must return to the ocean. I have unfinished business. I must find my friends and my family. I will call on the Kekken to help me." He looked across at Gero. "I was hoping you would still come with me."

"I did say that I would help you my friend, but I have also vowed to help these people rebuild their lives" explained Gero.

"You have already done more than enough for us" said Muyda. "With the threat from the Emperor gone, we can manage."

"Why do you need our help if you have an army of fish at your disposal?" asked Hanelore.

"I need you for the re-assuring friendship and positive encouragement you give" joked Var. Gero, Var and Muyda were still laughing long after Hanelore had left the room. Gero made his farewells and also left. Muyda noticed Var clutching his side as he stood.

"Is that still sore? You may have broken something." Said Muyda.

"A bit" replied Var.

"Take your shirt off and let me have a look" ordered Muyda. Var did as he was told. Var's body was a patchwork of black and green bruises pockmarked with cuts and grazes. Muyda examined his ribs. Var flinched as her cold hands touched his skin.

"I'm sorry" apologized Muyda.

"Your hands are cold that's all" explained Var.

"You took quite a beating" murmured Muyda.

"I have quite a talent for it" smiled Var. Muyda spun the young man around to see the injuries on his back. She stared dumbstruck at the small tattoo on his back. The striped camouflaged tattoos of his tribe finished around his shoulders, but in the centre of his back just below his neck was a small blurred tattoo. Muyda placed her finger on it.

"Where did you get this mark?" she asked.

"I'm not sure" said Var. "I've always had it I think." He heard footsteps and turned to see Muyda hurrying to leave the room. He shrugged his shoulders and lay down on the bed. No sooner had he shut his eyes, he fell sound asleep.

Set had been watching the violent storm from one of the thin windows. The winds had awoken the sea and it lashed massive waves against the harbour walls. He closed the shutters and heard the rain tapping at the wood. As he walked passed Muyda's room he heard faint sobs. He crept quietly in. She was sitting on the bed holding her head and crying softly.

"What is it?" he asked in his usual delicate way.

"My son" she sobbed. "Var is my son."

"How can that be?" asked Set. Muyda rubbed her eyes and looked up.

"Do you remember I told you that Dar and I had a child?"

"Yes I remember" said Set. "You had him taken away at birth to hide the secret from the Emperor."

"Yes we did. He was marked with the symbol of Shu on his back. Var has that same symbol."

"Have you told him?" enquired Set.

"No" said Muyda. "He must never know."

Chapter 9 – Vengeance

Mido flew through the plunge pool closely followed by his brother. They were gasping for breath and looked frightened by whatever it was they had encountered.

"Father!" shouted Mido.

Gednu hurried out from his sleeping pod to see what the commotion was about.

"They're here father! They are on the outskirts of the city."

"I knew it" cursed Gednu.

It had been many moons since he had led his family away from their doomed village. They had spoken to the elders in Beng Melea without much success so had moved on to the capital of the Enki Tribe, Montien Booma. Here Gednu had again spoken with the elders and the Helmsman on more than one occasion but they had been reluctant to hear his pleas. They were clearly disturbed by the aggressive action of the Eburus but they simply could not act. They had no means of crossing the Great Rift which meant the women of Antykia were truly lost. Gednu knew in his heart that this was true but had urged them to deploy defensive measures, increase patrols and alert all of the pods within the tribe. He could understand their reticence. After all, there had been peace beneath the ocean for as long as history had been recorded, but to do nothing when presented with the facts was in his opinion nothing short of stupidity.

Astur had backed him up but even with his testimony and the information on Rickron they still would not act. Gednu had managed to persuade them to send a party to their village to search for survivors. They found none. On their search towards the Rift they had found Astur floating silently, close to his last breath. They had brought him back to Booma and he had slowly recovered his physical strength and speech, although the right hand side of his face still remained slightly paralysed.

With the grave news that Mido had just relayed, Gednu felt vindicated in his protests but knew that was of little use. With what seemed like the entire Eburus tribe approaching the city they would need a miracle from Povian to save them.

Astur and Gednu listened intently as the young boys eagerly explained what they had seen.

"Why would they attack again?" questioned Astur.

"Perhaps this time they have come to stay rather than a swimming visit" suggested Gednu.

"Whatever the reason I will send them to the depths this time" said Astur through gritted teeth.

"You'll have your chance for vengeance; I hope the price will be worth paying."

The two men were disturbed from their conversation by splashing in the pool and one large Outrider climbed out. Astur went forward to meet him.

"Turem! It's good to see you" greeted Astur.

"Likewise my friend. I'm glad to see you have recovered. I wish it was under different circumstances that I was making this visit."

"What's happening?" asked Gednu.

"There has been no response from the outlying pods. We were in the process of sending a shoal to investigate when we got news of the Eburus gathering en masse. It looks as if you were right Master Gednu" offered Turem.

"I hope it's not too late" replied Gednu.

"I have come here with six other Outriders, the city has been mobilised and we are heading out to meet them. I was hoping you would join us" suggested Turem with a smile. Astur clasped him by the forearm and quickly gathered his gear. He tightened the buckles on his skin and slid two knives into each leg scabbard. He returned to the pool with a harpoon in each hand. Gednu and his two sons were already prepared and waiting.

The group slid into the water and headed out through the city pods. Astur could taste the anticipation of battle. He turned to face Turem.

<<FLANK>> he signed.

<<AGREE>> Turem signalled back.

They swam on at speed, the two boys sticking close to their father. They proceeded out of the city and along the uninhabited outer reaches. They kept low to the ground, keen to keep surprise on their side. As they neared the marker buoy to Swe Dagon they stopped and looked out across the gentle slopes approaching the city.

The ocean teemed with Eburus warriors all swimming towards the city. The majority of the Enki tribe had waited amongst the last of the outlying pods; they were new to the machinations of battle so were learning as they went. There seemed to be an everlasting pause before eventually the two sides clashed. It was a blur. Blood started to cloud the water and it soon became unclear what was happening. Astur moved as if ready to enter the fray. Gednu's hand held him back.

<<WAIT>> he signalled.

For what seemed like an age the group of warriors waited. Gednu nodded at his sons and in an instant they were off. The Outriders followed the two boys but struggled to keep up with their youthful pace. As they neared the battle they could see the small groups of Eburus warriors in neat lines slowly moving into the defenders.

They were arranged in small groups of ten soldiers, spread out in a line. The two outer men swam forward and launched their harpoons and then swam to the centre of the group. Then the next two flanking warriors would repeat the action. The tactic kept an almost constant stream of harpoons on the defenders and when all had been launched the squad advanced on the survivors with their knives drawn. It was a formidable ploy and many Enki tribesmen were already floating lifelessly in the crimson tide. They had not however expected an attack from the rear.

Mort and Mido reached the enemy line first and rammed home their harpoons. They drew their second barbless staves and proceeded to stab the unprotected warriors in the back. Five enemy combatants floated dead when Astur and the others arrived. Astur had not waited to reach stabbing distance; he had launched his harpoon whilst still swimming. The razor sharp barb had erupted through the man's chest sending a plume of blood into the water. Within a matter of moments the group had slaughtered the Eburus squad.

Their surprise and their victory had been short lived. The next enemy group along witnessed the slaughter and made to intercept them. Astur swirled, throwing his body to one side as a harpoon raced through the water. Despite his quick action the harpoon grazed his shin as it passed leaving a cloudy red line along it. He looked ahead at the man who had leased it. He was swimming full tilt with both knives drawn. He swam head on presenting as small a target as possible to Astur.

Astur swam towards him and then span onto his back; he kicked his legs up and shot down. As he did so he thrust his harpoon up towards the oncoming warrior. Despite his enemy's attempt to dodge the glinting tip, the barb ripped through his black and white skin and into his flesh. The strike tore through his abdominal wall and the man gulped and clutched at the wound trying to keep it together. His futile gesture was short lived as Astur rammed his knife into the dying man's throat. He withdrew the knife and slashed through his breather pipe. The sudden burst of oxygen turned the dead man over, blood and entrails flowing into the ocean.

Gednu fought with his two sons at his side. He lunged out with his spear which was much longer than the average harpoon as it was designed to stab rather than throw. The weapon was hollow and had a long cord running through the inside which ended in a hoop at the handle. As the deadly spear pierced the body of its next victim, Gednu yanked the hoop and the two previously flush barbs at the tip shot out trapping the struggling warrior. Gednu reeled the spear towards him hand over hand and as the hooked warrior drew close the two boys swam out stabbing furiously at the helpless tribesman. Gednu released the barbs and the fallen warrior floated away.

The small group of outriders grew in size and stature as they made their way slowly into the flank of the Eburus line, their numbers swelling as the defending townspeople joined their ranks. Despite their success the group had only made a tiny dent in the vast numbers of Eburus.

As Astur dived towards another warrior he heard a low grumble which sent a tremor through the water. The Eburus warriors looked at each other before turning and swimming away in retreat. The Enki tribesmen thrust their harpoons upwards in triumph, some choosing to throw them after the retreating horde.

The small group of outriders swam to the nearest pod and surfaced in the pool. They sat exhausted around the edge. They had lost only one of their initial number.

"We beat them father!" exclaimed Mort.

"For now we have my son. I fear this was just the first wave."

"I agree" said Turem. "They will be back; we must be ready."

*

Var was somewhat sad to be leaving the busy fortress. The violent storms during the night had battered the island but he had awoken to a bright blue sky and was keen to be on his way. He had made his goodbyes to an overly emotional Muyda and boarded Hanelore's ship along with Gero.

Hanelore had been busy studying his charts and looking at his navigational globe, whilst Var and Gero had tied off the sails. They were sat at the prow of the ship as it cut its way through the waves.

"So little Var, what will you do when we reach the place where your woman is held?" asked the giant.

"She is not my woman" said Var. "Least not yet anyway." He was avoiding the question. Gero just raised his eyebrows.

"I'll free her and the rest of them" said Var confidently.

"And how will you do that may I ask?" questioned Gero.

"You said you would help me" replied Var sarcastically.

"You've more chance convincing the old goat to dive beneath the surface than getting me to do it."

"You're not scared are you?" taunted Var.

"Course he is" interrupted Hanelore. "He fell overboard when he was a youngster; he has never got over it."

Var looked at the big man who seemed to blush at his weakness.

"I'll be OK" said Var patting the giant's arm. Hanelore laughed out loud as he returned to his charts.

With the winds in their favour the trio made good progress. Hanelore slowed the boat and ordered Var and Gero to drop the sails. Hanelore took a small metal sphere connected to a knotted line and tossed it over the edge. He fed the line through his hands counting the knots as they descended.

"This is my best guess" stated Hanelore. "The Great Chasm is ahead so this should be roughly the area you need."

"It will be close enough" said Var "My friends will know where to go if I can contact them."

"Ah yes your fish friends" laughed Hanelore. Var readied himself, checked his breather and put on his flippers.

"You will wait for me?" queried Var.

"Just put a marker at the end of the anchor line and you'll find your way back to us boy" said Hanelore.

"We'll be here" said Gero reassuringly.

Var sat on the rail of the boat and fell backwards into the water. He found the anchor line and made his way down to the sea bed. He grabbed the small charm around his neck, held his breath and blew into the small trinket. The bead inside spun but it didn't seem to make a sound. He replaced his breather and set off taking a lingering look back at his marker flag.

He had swum for some distance when feint shapes started to immerge from the gloom. As he drew closer he could make them out as pods similar to that of his own tribe. He was about to enter the nearest one when he became aware of something behind him. He turned and jumped as the kekken swished its tail to stop. Behind the creature a seething mass of animals slowly came into view. Var approached the animal and held out his arms to the creature. The kekken obliged and placed its thumbs on Var's wrists.

[You called us brother] The thought thumped into Var's mind. He hadn't been as ready for the shock of the mind link as he had hoped.

[I believe this is where the women of my tribe are being held] projected Var.

[Yes] came the reply.

[You want us to kill your own kind] The creature had read his mind but was confused.

[No] blurted Var [Just the Eburus, the ones wearing black and white]

[They are still your own kind?]

[No, they are nothing like me] retorted Var. With that the kekken removed the link and the tribesman jerked back in the water. The mass of creatures flooded past him and he turned to follow into the Eburus city of Symerna.

The city was strangely deserted albeit for a few elderly tribesmen. They were quickly ripped to pieces by the dark tide of kekken. As they drew closer to the Rift Var could see huge plumes of white mist and debris rising up through the water. Near the edge of the rift wall were several enormous hydrothermal vents. They were ushering super heated water from the bowels of the planet into the ocean. Var was awestruck by the natural phenomenon.

The Eburus had constructed metal collars around each of the underwater geysers, and Var could see how they used them to cross the Black River. The giant cages that they had used when they attacked his village were placed snugly into the mouth of the chimney stack. The pressure built quickly and then sent the cage on its angled trajectory across the Rift like a cork popping from a bottle. Each cage was connected via a giant chain to a winding drum anchored on the edge of the precipice. A geared handle at the side of the spool wound the cages back when they released their grip on the far edge. Var marvelled at the ingenious engineering that harnessed the power of the inner core.

The large black kekken swam up to face Var. He proffered his arms in communication once more. The mind link thumped into his thoughts once again.

[This is a poisoned place] came the thought from the creature.

[How so?] asked Var.

[These vents spew poison into the water. It is not safe to live among them]

It suddenly all started to make sense. This was the reason the Eburus had attacked. It also could explain the lack of people in the city as the Eburus must be out hunting again. But for what? More women or a new home? Whatever the reason it will be their last hunt thought Var unaware he was still connected to the kekken.

[You would still pursue them and kill them?] came the question.

[I would ask that you accompany me, that is all. I do not want you to kill for me again] replied Var.

[As you wish brother] and with that he released Var from the link.

A leathery talon wrapped around his wrist and guided him back into the city. He followed the creature to a pod as large as his village nest. He slowly surfaced in the pool and saw the macabre prison inside. The women lay subdued in their cages. Most showed signs of abuse and some had given up the fight for life completely. They stirred as the long haired tribesman climbed from the pool. Var's eyes eagerly scanned the cages searching for Bronsur. He saw her huddled in a ball in the corner of a cage.

"Bron!" he blurted. Bronsur started at the sound of her name and looked up to see the welcome sight of her beloved. Tears welled in her eyes.

"I said I would come for you" he said sadly.

"You took your time" she said forcing a smile. Var flinched at the sight of her broken teeth. Anger renewed itself in his heart. He found the keys nearby and proceeded to unlock the cages. He stooped into the cage and knelt down. He pulled Bronsur into his embrace. She sobbed in relief into his shoulder and Var cursed himself for not coming sooner. If he had he may well have prevented the events that took place here. He knew that was untrue but wished it all the same. He slowly helped Bronsur from the cage.

"My name is Var" he said loudly. "Most of you know me; I am the son of Gednu. I survived the attack by the Eburus but I was lost in the Black River. I am sorry I did not get here sooner." He saw the looks on their faces and knew that they bore no grudge against him.

"Much has changed in my world and yours in the passing moons. Some changes you may find hard to understand but if we are to survive this then you must try to accept it."

"What do you mean?" said Bronsur holding his arm.

"I have travelled to the surface of the ocean and beyond. I have walked upon the land above the waves and breathed fresh air. I have looked into the stars and felt the warmth of Shu on my face. "

There were gasps and mumblings and Bronsur stared wide-eyed at the tribesman.

"There is nothing to fear. You must trust me and follow me to the surface where my friends are awaiting us."

The women, although in shock at Var's revelation were in no state to argue and most were simply grateful that their ordeal was at an end. A sudden scream rocked Var and he spun to see the source of the noise. A kekken had emerged through the pool.

"Its okay!" shouted Var trying to placate the newly terrified gathering.

"They mean you no harm." Var walked to the pool and knelt. He signed to the creature.

<<WE COME>>

The creature, understanding his gesture, slipped beneath the surface of the water. He looked back at Bronsur who was still staring open mouthed. After gathering as many breathers as he could find Var led the women out from the city and back towards his marker. They arrived at the anchor line, some of the party clearly suffering from the exertion of the swim. He looked at Bronsur.

<<SAFE>> he signed. She squeezed his hand tightly as they rose along the line towards the surface. One by one the Enki women broke the surface into the bright light around the hull of the giant's boat. Only after Var had removed his breather did they follow suit. The giant outstretched hand of Gero plucked Var nimbly from the water. The dumbstruck women followed quickly after.

"I feel there is much more to your story than you have told us" said Bronsur staring up at the massive stature of Gero.

"There is a lot to tell" he smiled. "This is my friend Gero and his father Hanelore." Both giants nodded politely. Bronsur was struggling to take it all in and was still mesmerised by Gero.

"But he is..."

"Big" finished Var with a laugh.

"I would have said portly" interrupted Hanelore. "He eats too much." The jovial mood relaxed the women. Var approached the giant.

"You know you said I couldn't possibly drag you beneath the water?" proposed Var.

"Yes" said Gero hesitantly.

"I need your help with something; I cannot do it without you." He pointed overboard.

"Down there."

After several false starts, Gero had finally stopped holding his breath and started to breathe through the mouthpiece. He followed closely behind Var trying to keep pace in the alien environment. By the time the two men had reached the city Gero had found a rhythm to his swimming action and was beginning to enjoy his time beneath the waves.

Var led him to where the huge chains disappeared out across the void. The spool was twice the height of the giant and was secured to the bedrock by four equally large pins. The pins passed through the base plate of the winding mechanism and were secured by another intersecting clip. Var swam down to the fastener and pointed at it to Gero. The giant nodded his understanding and both men scoured the area for tools. Var returned with a heavy metal bar and Gero a metal handled forge hammer. Var held his metal bar against the securing clip and Gero swung the hammer. Despite the friction of the water the hammer blow sent the pin bouncing out across the plate. They repeated the process on the other three pins. As the last one fell the winch unit lurched upwards slightly but remained in place.

The two friends worked their way along the winch line, sabotaging each machine as they went. The exhausted pair surfaced some time later next to the expectant boat load. Bronsur rushed to meet Var.

"Hanelore has been telling us about your adventures" she said excitedly. Var glanced across at the old giant, who winked back.

"Oh has he?" said Var.

"He told us that you are king of those creatures that we saw" continued Bronsur.

"He has a tendency to exaggerate" replied Var. "Those creatures are called Kekken. They are intelligent and are simply helping me to repay a favour. There is much I still don't understand about them."

"You can tell me all about it when we get home" said Bronsur. Var remained silent trying to hide the look of concern on his face.

*

The group of outriders had not had to wait long for the next attack. They had been alerted to the new advance and had taken up positions with the rest of the Enki force amongst the pods. They had hoped the buildings may afford them some protection from the deadly Eburus harpoons. This was not to be.

The blurred lines of the Eburus slowly started to sharpen as they approached the city. There was something different this time about the formation. They were not split into small groups but seemed to form an impenetrable line. At the front of the line there were individual warriors. They seemed from a distance to be much larger than normal.

The Enki warriors waited with trepidation as the large warriors slowly approached. As they neared, the reason for their tired advance became apparent. The lumbering warriors walked along the seabed rather than swimming like the rest of the enemy force. They were encased from head to toe in rusty metal suits and carrying a strange looking device with both arms. Bubbles streamed from a duct on the back of the suit and Astur could make out the eyes of the man encased behind a glass plate on the helmet. All along the line these metal goliaths advanced, the remainder of the Eburus number keeping a short distance behind. The confused Enki tribesmen looked at each other with puzzled expressions.

As the first inhuman figure approached, a group of warriors swam out to confront it. They hurled their harpoons with deadly force and accuracy but the razor sharp projectiles only bounced off the armour plating. In a panic they drew their knives and descended on the walking menace. As they did, the armoured Eburus lifted his strange weapon and aimed it at the oncoming men. He pulled a trigger and a weighted net shot from the machine trapping and snaring the stunned fighters. The trapped men tried desperately to free themselves but their movements only further entangled them. One hacked at the net with his knife but the blade would not cut the wire netting.

Another lone Eburus warrior swam in behind his comrade and attached a hook and line to the net. No sooner had he done so the horde behind him dragged the catch back towards them. As it reached the pulsing tide of black and white killers, they swarmed over their enemies in a frenzy stabbing their harpoons into the captured men.

Astur felt a sickness rising in his gut as he witnessed the same scene unfolding along the line. The armoured point men continued their unfaltering advance into the Enki lines, reloading a new net after each catch. Turem turned to Astur and signed.

<<ATTACK>>

<<YES>> replied Astur. Gednu saw the sign and swam forward to grab Astur by the arm.

<<STAY>> he signalled.

<<DEFEND>>

Astur looked into the older man's eyes and Gednu knew there was no stopping him. He watched with his two sons as the group of Outriders swam out to meet their foe. All along the line the other Enki shoals were following suit. They had ventured it a better option to attack than to wait to be captured and slaughtered by the advancing metal nightmares.

Astur's shoal avoided the nearest armoured catcher and swam over him and on towards the dark tide of warriors beyond. As they approached, the Eburus retreated for a second time. Astur and Turem kicked hard, eager to engage the enemy. As they closed the waiting traps were activated. Huge nets that had been laid across the sea bed shot upwards catching the unaware swimmers in its embrace. The sand swirled and visibility reduced but only for those trapped. The Eburus once again closed in with murderous intent.

Gednu looked out on the hopeless slaughter and cursed the Eburus with his every being. His focus was thrown as Mort grabbed his arm and pointed towards the approaching metal warrior. The warrior had dropped his net weapon and was advancing with a long straight bladed sword in his rusty grip.

The trio swam to meet the juggernaut. As they closed Gednu looked into the glass visor and recognised the murderous stare of Rickron. In this brief moment of recognition Rickron had lashed out with his blade. It had cut through Gednu's suit but luckily only caused a shallow wound across his stomach. Mort and Mido swarmed Rickron thudding knife blows harmlessly into his armour. Rickron swung his metal arm and struck Mido around the side of the head spinning him away.

Gednu charged. He hit Rickron low, smashing into his knees with his shoulder. The force of the impact started to topple Rickron who fought desperately with his arms to keep himself upright. Mort followed his father's lead and body slammed the iron warrior. Rickron fell and thudded into the seaweed.

Gednu quickly pressed the advantage and jumped onto his sword arm pinning it and Rickron to the seabed. His two sons appeared at his side, knives drawn. Gednu simply placed a single finger on the glass visor. The boys obeyed. Mido's knife point struck the glass and it cracked slightly. The duo repeated the onslaught until Mido's final blow smashed the glass and the knife popped the eyeball on its way through Rickron's eye socket embedding itself deep in his brain. The two boys helped their father to his feet. When he looked out to the battle he had to blink rapidly to establish what he was seeing was not a dream.

The Eburus were in full retreat as thousands of black shapes darted through the water towards them. Var led the army of kekken towards the terrified warriors. The kekken had not attacked as Var had promised. They had not needed to. The terror of their sudden appearance had caused all of the Eburus force to turn and run. They swam for their lives, desperate to reach the safety of their cages on the edge of the rift.

Var looked on as the frightened men clambered aboard the cages and wound in the retaining hooks. One by one the hooks released their hold on the bedrock and the iron cages swung away, caught by the constant pull of the Black River. Var watched as the warriors screamed silently, their cages plummeting into the dark depths. The confused Eburus did not understand how their lifeline had faltered. Var stayed and waited as the last of the cages was torn from the edge into oblivion.

The large kekken approached the young man who offered up his arms to the mind bond.

[Is your thirst for vengeance sated brother] came the predicted question.

[We all make our own destiny brother. Just as you and I have arrived at this point they too chose their end the day they killed my kinsmen and tortured our women] projected Var.

[We still have much to understand. We each live and die for each other] came the response.

[You are nobler creatures than us] replied Var. The creature released the bond and stared face to face with its human brother. It traced its claw along Var's scar and then turned and left. The thousands of assembled kekken disappeared with him.

Chapter 10 – Prophecy

Gero was still marvelling at the colossal underwater structure. The immense nest of the Enki was the hub of the tribe and was the dominant building in Booma. The huge bones of some unknown sea creature arced above even the giant Gero. The white of the polished bones was in stark contrast against the outer plates. Unlike most nests the plunge pool was in the centre. Around the pool were tiered seats forming an amphitheatre. A raised dais punctuated the pool. This ancient building had seen the history of the ocean tribes unfold.

Var stood next to Gero on the central dais nervously moving from foot to foot and unsure of what to do with his hands. The giant noticed the small man's anxiety.

"Relax little Var" he said softly.

"That's easy for you to say" complained Var. "It's not you that has to address the elders of your tribe. What if they don't want to hear what I have to say?"

"After you saved them from the brink of annihilation I am sure they will hear you out at the very least" countered Gero. "Say what you feel little man, that is all you can do. That proved a good tactic when you spoke to the Titan." Gero winked.

The nest slowly filled with what remained of the Enki tribe. Most were carrying an injury of some description. They all took their seats in silence. Var mistook the respectful reserve as a mark of respect for the recently fallen.

An elderly tribesman stood and walked out along the small path to the dais where Var and Gero were waiting. His long wet white hair draped over his fading tattoos. He carried a long bone walking stick set at the top with a pearlescent shell. He tapped it gently on the stone floor.

"I am Jarey Son-Circ Bay-Enki. I have been the proud Helmsman of our tribe for many long seasons. In the recent carnage we have lost over two thirds of our people against the murderous Eburus. My inaction and blindness is the reason the death toll is so high." The old man lifted his walking stick and brought it down over his knee snapping it in two. He took the shell from the broken cane and turned to Var. He knelt down and offered the sacred relic to the young man. As Var reluctantly took the shell from Jarey, the old man turned and shouted.

"Prince of the ocean."

The assembled crowd simultaneously thumped their feet and harpoons against the floor. The tumultuous noise stunned the already tense Var. As the noise abated Var remained motionless. Gero stepped forward and bent to whisper in his ear.

"I think this is where you say something."

The young tribesman jerked back to reality.

"I am Var Son-Gednu Bay-Enki." His voice was slightly croaky. He cast a swift glance at Gero who smiled back.

"I am sad that Jarey thinks he must renounce his position. No one could have foreseen the evil of the Eburus. It is now in this time of crisis that a strong leader is needed." Var turned to the old man. "Jarey, will you not reconsider?" The old man looked puzzled by the question.

"It is you who lead us now" he said clearly. This sentiment was again echoed around the nest by cheers and shouts. Var stepped forward and raised his arms. The din slowly faded.

"I am honoured you think me worthy" said Var. "And this makes what I have come here to say even more difficult." He cleared his throat. "Although I was raised as a child of the ocean, the events of the past moons have changed me. I have broken through the surface and breathed fresh air above. I have walked on dry land and seen the ocean break on the rocks. I have seen the ancient ruins of mighty cities built by our forebears and I have felt the warmth of Shu against my face." Var bowed his head. Gero stepped forward and patted him on the shoulder.

"Finish it little man" he whispered sternly.

"There is another world above. A world which we believed was forbidden to us. But I have seen its beauty and it is a place to which I must return. I am not the Prince of the ocean. I am simply a son of Shu."

There was complete silence. Gednu, who sat in the front row, squeezed the hand of his wife as a lone tear trickled down her cheek. What their son had just announced contravened all the laws and legends of the ocean people. Gero stepped forward.

"I am Gero of the Magta. My people have lived on this planet before the time of the half-light. We are now a dying race as we have been too stubborn and conceited to adapt to change. This is the zenith of your people. You must now decide your future path and that of your descendants."

*

As Hanelore winched in the anchor Var stared out over the stern at the ropes dangling behind the boat. Those who were fit enough were attached to long ropes that trailed out like trawler nets behind the boat. A sea of expectant faces greeted him as they started to pull gently through the water. He had been amazed that so many had decided to follow him. Only a handful of elderly, infirm and devotees had stayed behind. Even the seriously wounded were crammed into the great yacht. Most were still gazing out at the white caps and the speeding clouds above.

Mort and Mido were high up in the rigging. Hanelore had given them specific instructions which they were only too pleased to follow. Var noticed Astur talking to his father. He desperately wanted to speak to him, but the images of

Astur floating lifelessly remained in his memory and made him feel awkward. Bronsur looked over and caught his eye.

"Var!" she shouted. She beckoned him over. As he approached, Astur stood and turned. The two men held each other's gaze. Astur stepped forward and embraced his friend. Var returned the gesture.

"I'm truly sorry" said Astur through a slightly distorted mouth.

"We've all lost a great deal" said Var. "You more than most."

"You don't know what I did" offered Astur.

"You're here now, nothing else matters my friend" replied Var.

The slimline craft tore through the ocean carrying and dragging its refugee cargo with it. Gero had developed a young entourage. The children of the tribe were fascinated by the giant man and ignored the shoals of leaping shalluki to follow their new idol.

"Ho!" came the shout from high up in the rigging and Hanelore looked up to Mort and Mido. He pointed his glass scope in the direction they were signalling.

"Is it Imercia?" asked Var.

"Patience my little friend" replied Hanelore.

"Gero!" shouted Hanelore. "Take the helm." The old giant picked his way through the Enki cargo and out onto the prow closely followed by Var. As they looked ahead the contours of the island became visible. Excitement spread through the Enki like wildfire. All the while Hanelore had kept the scope firmly pressed against his eye.

"What is it?" insisted Var. Hanelore lowered the eyeglass and he looked greyer than normal.

"A nightmare" he said simply. Var grabbed the eyeglass and held it up. He focussed. His hands started to shake and he eventually lowered the scope. He urged and grabbed at his stomach and then heaved the contents over the side.

"Hard to port" ordered Hanelore. Gero spun the ship's wheel and the great vessel lurched to the left. The passengers could sense the unease and the euphoria was replaced by nervous whispers. As Var followed the old giant back to the helm Gednu grabbed his arm.

"What is it son?" he asked.

"I'll tell you all as soon as we land" replied Var. Hanelore relayed the news of what he had seen to Gero. The giant cursed under his breath.

"What have I done" pleaded Var. "I have brought my tribe from one torment to another."

"Destiny is littered with obstacles" said Hanelore. "How a person masters them determines the path he treads."

"It's not time for philosophy" snapped Var.

"What will you do then boy?" argued Hanelore. "Run or stand and face your demons?"

"You know the answer to that" said Var.

"Then let's stop arguing and start preparing" stated Hanelore.

*

The great yacht dropped its anchor at the opposite end of the island far from the fortress. They had stayed way out to sea and had only headed landward when they were shielded by the hills of Imercia. The Enki had disembarked and those that had been towed gladly dropped their breathers and clambered up the beach. In the excitement of landing and the myriad of new sights and sounds the earlier uneasy reactions of Var and the giants had been forgotten.

Var climbed up onto the rocks and waited patiently as the jubilant gathering turned their attentions on him.

"I know I promised you a new start and a new life on this land" started Var. "It seems as if the Gods do not want peace for us. We left this place with new found friends rebuilding their lives and I had hoped we would return and join them. Before that can happen it seems we must fight one last battle."

The tribe watched as a heavily armoured Gero bearing his massive golden axe and Hanelore carrying a long leather tube made their way up the beach. Chaos erupted and arguments broke out in the crowd. There was a loud 'chink' as Gero thundered his axe into the rock. The startled crowd turned to the giant warrior.

"This is not what you or we expected, but it is, as it is. If this is to be your new home you must earn that right. One last obstacle stands before you and the great ocean lies behind. Your choice is a simple one." Var bounded over to the armoured giants and Gero saw the look of disappointment on his face.

"There is no time for sentiment" defended Gero. "We must wipe the Dumon disease from this place once and for all, or die trying."

"I know" resigned Var. "I am with you..."

"And so are we!" added Astur and Gednu. The two men were backed by the entire tribe.

"Take this little Var" said Hanelore. He gave him the leather package. "I will return to the boat and see what weapons we have on board."

"What is it?" asked Var.

"It is the Nightsigh" replied Hanelore as he waded back out towards the boat. Gero and Var climbed a rocky crag and walked a short distance down onto a small plateau. The golden fields of ripe crops stretched out before them. Beyond that was the imposing fortress. What they seen had from the boat was now clearly visible. Hanging from the walls on inverted crosses were the remnants of the Murai. The tortured and bloody bodies decorated the walls like rotten fruit. Beneath the fortress a few haggard survivors were harassed by Reavers as they struggled to bring in the harvest.

On the top of the curtain wall the two friends could see the white armour of the Emperor reflecting like a beacon in the bright light.

"It is time for the Nightsigh to sing its song" muttered Gero. Var handed the package to the giant who started to unwrap it.

"What is it?" asked Var.

"It is a family heirloom. An ancient weapon that has been handed down through the generations. I have not used it in anger since I was a young boy." Gero gently removed two curved black limbs and an intricately carved handle. He attached the two limbs to the handle to form a huge recurve bow. He placed the bow between his legs and applied pressure to one end enabling him to hook on the bowstring. The string slotted into the horn notches and Gero thumbed it. The bow hummed like a musical instrument. The handle had two metal lengths sticking out on either side each threaded with knurled wheels.

The giant withdrew a long black case from the bag and flicked open the catches. Inside, the box was divided into three compartments. He took out one of the long black arrow shafts, itself almost the same height as Var, and screwed in a flight. He then pondered over the tip selection. Finally Gero selected a vicious looking barb and attached it to the other end.

"That will never reach the fortress will it?" questioned Var.

"This is no ordinary bow my little friend" replied Gero. He turned the massive bow on its side and notched the arrow. He turned it vertically and adjusted the wheels on either side.

"That should do it" he muttered. As he lifted the bow he drew the arrow back to his chin. The bow began to resonate. As he adjusted the angle of the bow the pitch of the hum increased. As his aim got higher so did the pitch until eventually it stopped altogether. At that point Gero released his fingers and the arrow zinged into the distance.

*

Lord Senn strode along the crenellated walkway looking down on the returning Murai with disgust. He had enjoyed the brief slaughter when they had arrived, but it had ended so quickly. The Murai defences had quickly collapsed under his guided assault even though his forces had been substantially depleted during the storms at sea. He had decided to stay on the island to personally oversee the rebuilding of the Lexan gate and ensure that this time the food supplies made it back to Son-Gebshu. After only a couple of rotations he was becoming bored.

The Emperor suddenly jumped back as the Reaver in front of him inexplicably flew backwards off the wall. The crumpled body of the Reaver lay in a heap in the courtyard below. A black arrow jutted from his chest. Before he could react, a second soldier was smashed from the wall. He hit the inner tower wall behind before falling onto the ground.

Var was looking through the scope.

"That's amazing. I can't believe it will fire that far let alone hit anything" said Var gasping.

"Thanks for your confidence" smiled Gero. "The bow has incredible power. It took me many seasons to master it. As for the arrows they have a trick all of their own. They are sound sensitive, especially the repeating rhythm of a heartbeat."

"Oh" said Var.

"Plus I am a really good marksman" said Gero.

"Why do you think the Kekken told me the Emperor would be killed in the storms?" asked Var changing the subject to the real issue on his mind.

"Did they say that?" Gero shrugged. "Maybe they don't know everything" suggested the giant. "Or maybe they are using you more than you realise."

"Do you think so?" asked Var.

"I really don't know" said Gero. "All I know is that something that deadly and intelligent scares me, and that's not easy." The two men looked back towards the noise coming over the hill and saw the Enki tribe led by Hanelore.

"How many have you bagged?" asked the old giant.

"Only two, little Var has been distracting me" Replied Gero.

Var looked at his people. They were all armed in some way, with either their own harpoons and knives or strange blades and pikes, probably from Hanelore's collection. They all carried long pieces of plank, which looked like they had recently been part of the ships decking.

"Is the ship still afloat?" asked Var.

"It's looking a little tattered" agreed Hanelore. Astur and Gednu approached the trio.

"Do we have a strategy of some kind?" enquired Astur.

"We need to stay clear of the wall mounted weapons" said Gero.

"Is that it?" exclaimed Gednu as he cast a worried glance at his son.

"They are well armoured and well disciplined fighters" said Var. "We must draw them out and present an easy target. Their over-confidence will be their weakness."

"Their over-confidence!" repeated Gednu.

"Trust me father this will work" assured Var.

"Better take a look at this" interrupted Hanelore. Var grabbed the looking glass and pointed it toward the fortress. Lord Senn was staring out over the wall holding what looked like Muyda in front of him.

"They are using the Murai as flesh shields" he said sadly. "We will make our move at first light."

*

As the great white disk of Shu climbed slowly above the horizon, Var looked along the line of Enki warriors. They stood motionless in the waist high corn field. Var glanced down at the new weapons in his hands. Hanelore had given them to him the previous night. The mattocks were

255

wider than a sword blade and three quarters of the way along the wide blade it curved forward like a scythe. Hanelore had explained how the forward weight of the blade provided a hugely powerful cut at the apex. He had assured him it would cleave through armour. He would soon find out. He curled his fingers around the leather bound handle and then held one of the mattocks aloft.

Hanelore had carefully mixed two pungent liquids together and poured them into a small glass vial. He handed it to Gero who screwed the small object to an arrow shaft. They saw Var's signal and he drew back the string to his chin once again. The bow hummed loudly. He raised the bow and as it fell silent he loosed the arrow. The arrow sailed high over the walls and broke onto the keep roof. On impact the vial smashed and the contents erupted into flames. The fiery liquid cascaded down between the tiles and ignited the dry rafters below. A second arrow landed on the roof of the courtyard buildings and was quickly engulfed in flame. Gero handed the Nightsigh to his father.

"Your turn now old man, and don't miss" ordered Gero.

"I'd have a job to miss, you fat ox" he laughed.

Lord Senn had not slept. He had investigated the arrows and could tell they were of ancient craftsmanship. He had no idea who was outside the fortress. For the first time since the initial landing he felt excited once more.

The roar of flame sent most of the soldiers scurrying into the courtyard. They looked up to see the keep roof ablaze. Some were struggling to douse the flames in the courtyard, but the water strangely seemed to only fuel the fire.

Lord Senn climbed the steps of the outer wall keeping the frail Muyda out in front of him. He yanked her by the throat and she choked.

"Coward" coughed Muyda. The Emperor looked out across the corn field and saw the line of warriors stood before him. He immediately recognised Var.

"You!" he shouted. His outburst made Muyda focus and she squinted through her bruised eyes. She saw her son standing defiant.

"I told you my son would kill you" she laughed deliriously, her mind rapidly unfolding. "The prophecy will come to fruition."

"What are you babbling about witch" barked the Emperor. "I have already told you both sons are dead."

"Maybe they are" smiled Muyda. "But that one isn't" and she pointed out to Var. Her deteriorated mind had just unwittingly signed Var's death warrant. Lord Senn spun her around in his arms and looked in her eyes.

"What do you mean?" he demanded. Muyda just laughed. The Emperor knew exactly what she meant.

"To arms!" he shouted as he descended the stone steps throwing Muyda from them as he went. She landed motionless in the dust.

The Reavers filed in behind their leader as they eagerly made their way under the fortress siege gate. As they walked across the fields they slowly picked up their pace into a jog. Lord Senn unhitched his hammers, keen to start the bloodletting.

Var and the single line of Enki warriors remained still, even as the first arrow from Hanelore's bow thumped a Reaver off his feet. Var looked over his shoulder and could see the solitary figure of Gero loping towards him. He had not expected them to attack quite so soon.

Arrow after arrow thudded into the now sprinting Dumonii. The losses did not slow their advance. As Gero reached the line Var issued the command and the remainder of the Enki tribe that had lain hidden on the ground stood up to show themselves. They now outnumbered the oncoming soldiers two to one. The advance slowed slightly as the Reavers saw their enemy suddenly multiply. Reading the slight pause, Var held his arm aloft and ran headlong towards the charging black tide. The Reavers stopped and in an organised manner, formed regimented lines un-holstering their nail guns. As they prepared to fire Var and his tribe took the wide planks of wood from their backs and slammed them into the dirt and crouched behind them. The combined whine of the nailgun compressors made Var's ears pop, as he tried to make himself as thin as possible. The metal spikes hammered into the makeshift wooden shields. The volley was constant and many shards found their targets.

The whine stopped. Var issued his next command. The crouching tribesmen now picked up their harpoons and spears and launched them at the enemy. One Reaver drew his sword and moved forward only to be pinned to the spot by a well thrown stave. The time for strategical moves was now over and the two sides clashed in close combat.

Var jumped in the air and thundered his foot into the nearest Reaver. His weight and speed sent the warrior flying backwards. He pressed his advantage and brought one of the mattocks down on his sprawling victim. The Reaver tried to block the attack but the forward sweeping blade sliced through his arm and buried itself deep into his heart. Var had to stand on the dead man's chest to lever the weapon free.

All along the line the Enki and the Reavers clashed. Var was flanked by Astur whilst his father and the twins held sway behind Gero, so that no-one could get behind the giant war machine. As Var ducked a vicious riposte he felt comfort in the fact that Gero was fighting on his side.

He deftly parried a wild slash with his left and then attacked with his right. He brought the mattock down in an arc over his head. The Reaver moved his small buckler to block the strike. The deadly weapon obliterated the shield and splintered the bones in the Reavers hand. He yelled in pain. Var brought his left weapon back into play with a low sweep. The curved blade chopping into the side of the soldier's knee. The weighty blade severed the leather armour and the tendons behind. The crippled warrior buckled and as he did, Var launched his knee into the face of his opponent. Var winced as the fighter's teeth broke on his knee.

Var looked up for his next target and stared squarely into the brooding eyes of the Emperor.

Gero had thundered into the ranks of the Reavers like a tsunami. The golden axe harvesting the stunned combatants like the corn they stood amongst. The Reavers had immediately backed away and tried to circle the giant. Gednu and the twins ran in behind to protect his back.

Gero wielded the great axe as if it was an extension of his being. Limbs and heads toppled with every swing as he moved through his repertoire of martial moves. Every so often a large black arrow would thud into a chest plate knocking the soldier back into their comrades. Some shots were a little too close for Gero's liking.

"Careful you old groat!" he cursed. Sweat started to run freely from his brow and in the instant he took to wipe it from his vision a well aimed spear breached his defences and sliced through his side. Without slowing, he swung the butterfly axe and sliced through the shaft of the attacking weapon and then brought it down flat onto the

Reaver's head, breaking his neck and disintegrating his skull. He drew the spear tip from his side. It had bit deeply between his ribcage.

Again the giant pressed into the enemy trying to force his way through the line to divide them. An upward swing of the axe cleaved the nearest Reaver's head from his body. His dead corpse sprayed Gero and the surrounding fighters with blood. Gero watched the head bounce into the cornfield. Ahead of him a terrified soldier had crouched down. He had his nail gun held out in front of him. Without looking where he was firing he squeezed the trigger. The metal spikes peppered Gero's leg. The surprise of the volley made him stumble and his blood stained axe fell onto the ground followed by the crash of the giant himself. Seeing the advantage, the Reavers broke forward eager to claim the scalp of the fallen giant.

Gednu and the twins backed by two more Enki warriors hurdled the prostrate figure and fought to keep the enemy tide from engulfing their hero. Gero grabbed the haft of his axe and used it to help him stand. His muscular frame was drenched in blood; much of it now was his own.

The Lord Emperor snarled at his opponent.

"I should have killed you when I had the chance."

"I agree" said Var. "Killing an unarmed man is much more your style."

The Emperor lashed out with a flurry of attacks with his hammers. Var knew how good he was and jumped back continually to avoid the devastating blows. He caught his foot on a fallen body and tripped backwards.

Lord Senn threw one of his hammers towards Var. The hammer hit the dirt where Var's head had just been. The weapon was attached to a small chain. He yanked his arm down and the war hammer flew back into his gauntleted grasp.

Var knew he was no match for the seasoned leader. He fought for an opening or something that would change his luck, but the Emperor was flawless. It was luck that kept the furious flurry of blows from finding their target. As the Emperor attacked again the metal hammerhead crashed into Var's shoulder. Pain exploded down his arm and he dropped the heavy mattock into the soil. Still fighting, he blocked the next attack but the follow up blow splintered his knee. The Emperor withdrew the hammer spike and Var collapsed. As the Emperor strode over to his victim Var lashed out with his remaining mattok. The razor sharp blade clacked against Lord Senn's left greave. The blow smashed the armour and toppled the Emperor. As he fell, a black arrow went winging by and thumped into the ground nearby. Var swore. His blow had just saved the Emperor.

Lord Senn ripped the broken greave and tossed it aside. He jumped and landed with one foot pinning Var's arm. He swung his hammer and the spike punctured Var's arm pinning it to the ground. The Emperor stood and glared down at his quarry.

"You can kill me" spat Var. "But you have lost the day."

The Emperor looked around and it was true. Only a few pockets of Reavers were providing any resistance; the Enki were clearly in ascendance. For the first time Var saw a flicker of uncertainty on the Emperor's face.

Astur was struggling with a dead Reaver who had fallen on top of him, his short sword buried deep in the man's torso. He rolled and shrugged the lifeless body to one side. He looked across and saw Var lying on the floor.

Astur drew the sword from the dead man and hurled it at the Emperor. The sword clattered harmlessly off Lord Senn's ceramic armour. Astur searched the ground for a replacement weapon. He grasped the handle of an Enki harpoon and rose to face his oncoming enemy. He tightened his grip around the weapon and held it ready to jab. As the Emperor closed he rammed the harpoon towards his throat. The Emperor jumped and span, the barbed tip thrusting harmlessly into the air. With his remaining hammer held firm in his outstretched arm, he pounded it into the side of Astur's skull. The Enki warrior toppled into the dirt. The Emperor casually strolled back to his captive.

"A friend of yours" he chuckled as he looked back towards the dead body of Astur. Var said nothing. He could hear a loud noise coming from the fortress. The Emperor too looked up on hearing the sound. There were regular thumps and the familiar chink of armour. The thumping subsided as dozens of black clad Reavers poured from the fortress gate. The remaining Enki warriors retreated slightly as the Reaver reinforcements streamed out.

"It seems as if I get to kill you and win the day my young ocean friend" said the Emperor. "With your death the prophecy will finally die alongside you."

"You talk too much" said Var through bloody teeth.

"I agree" came a voice from behind the Emperor. An armoured fist slammed into the surprised Emperor's face twisting him from his feet and sending him sprawling into the dirt.

"The time for talking is long past" said Vas-Sem. The Dominator descended on the scrambling Emperor, his hammer blows exploding against Lord Senn's armour. The pauldron splintered as the hammerhead hit. Vas-Sem's second blow found the weak spot between the cuirass and the back plate, cracking the Emperor's ribcage. Lord Senn dropped his remaining weapon and spat bloody phlegm onto the ground.

"My son" he coughed. "You don't understand."

"Oh I understand perfectly" replied Vas-Sem. He circled both hammers turning each point inward as he did.

The two spikes crunched into the Emperor's temples. Vas-Sem released his grip and let his father crumple to the floor. The Emperor's Reavers remained still as did Gero and the Enki, awaiting the newcomer's next move. He strode to where Var lay.

"This world has been a bane on our civilisation. It has distracted us from our true goals. I will make our fading people great once more, and the first step in that process is to rid ourselves of this planet. Destroy the gate after we have passed through" commanded Vas-Sem. "This is where our destinies divide ocean man. I hope for your sake we never meet again."

The new Emperor of Son-Gebshu turned and left the battle.

Epilogue

Var looked out from the fortress walls at the thick black smoke billowing from the huge funeral pyre. The smoke rose up into the sky, obscuring the white glow of the setting Shu. The giant hand of Gero steadied Var as he attempted to move his splinted leg.

"This is all my doing" said Var.

"Maybe" answered Gero with a shrug.

"Aren't you supposed to re-assure me and tell me that my actions were unavoidable or something sage like that" questioned Var. The giant laughed and stroked the bony ridges on his scalp.

"Your hand was forced in the decisions you made. You have nothing to be ashamed of. There have been great losses, that I cannot deny, but you have created new hope and brought about a new dynasty for your people. History will remember you this way."

"That's much better!" laughed Var.

Lightning Source UK Ltd.
Milton Keynes UK
UKOW04f1518260615

254186UK00002B/111/P